PRAYER AND PARABLE

D0862777

PAUL MALISZEWSKI

PRAYER AND PARABLE

ALBANY · NEW YORK

The stories in this collection were originally published, sometimes in different form, in the following:

Black Warrior Review, *Bomb*, *Colorado Review*, *Fence*, *Gettysburg Review*, *McSweeney's*, *Mid-American Review*, *Mississippi Review*, *Notre Dame Review*, *One Story*, *Rain Crow*, *Salmagundi*, *StoryQuarterly*, *Verse*, *Vice*, and *Western Humanities Review*. "Parable of Another's Shoes" and "Parable of the Thread" appeared as "Prayer against the Tyranny of Another's Shoes" and "Prayer for the Strength of Thread," respectively, in the 2000 *Pushcart Prize* anthology. "Parable of the Experts and Their Ways" appeared as "Prayer against the Experts and Their Ways" in the 2003 *Pushcart Prize* anthology and was reprinted in *Harper's Magazine*. "Prayer for the Appearance of Something German" was reprinted in *Verse 1995–2004: The Second Decade*. Several of these stories also appeared in *The Book of Prayer*, a limited-edition chapbook. The author thanks Michael Martone, Elise Proulx, and Rebecca Wolff.

Copyright © 2011 by Paul Maliszewski
All rights reserved

Fence Books is a project of Fence Magazine, Incorporated, which is funded in part by support from the New York State Council on the Arts and the National Endowment for the Arts, along with the generous sponsorship of the New York State Writers Institute and the University at Albany. Many thanks to these friends and to all Friends of Fence.

Fence Books are distributed by Consortium Book Sales & Distribution (cbsd.com) and printed in Canada by Printcrafters, Inc. (printcraftersinc.com)

Design and typography by Michael Russem

Library of Congress Cataloguing in Publication Data
    Maliszewski, Paul
    Prayer and Parable/Paul Maliszewski

Library of Congress Control Number: 2011920294

ISBN 13: 978-1-934200-44-5

FIRST EDITION
10 9 8 7 6 5 4 3 2

To Hadley

Attention, taken to its highest degree, is the same thing as prayer. It presupposes faith and love.

Absolutely unmixed attention is prayer.

—SIMONE WEIL

I will open my mouth in parables; I will utter things which have been kept secret from the foundation of the world.

—Matthew 13:35

CONTENTS

PRAYER AND PARABLE

PRAYER AGAINST THE FORCE OF HABIT

THE ARGUMENT started pretty much the minute she came home. He had decided to stay at her place while she went out, intending to get some work done, but instead he puttered about. He picked up her shoes and took them to the closet. He washed a few dishes. He flipped through a magazine, but put it down when he realized he was reading captions without looking at the photos. He lay in bed looking at the ceiling, crossing and uncrossing his legs at the ankles. Then he got up and straightened things. He thought of putting some music on, which seemed like a grand idea, perfect, really, to have something to sing along with, to listen to, to make the time go, but the thought no sooner achieved this clarity than it faded and was replaced by something else—a pressing need to water the plants, inspiration to make the bed, the notion, from nowhere apparent, that a cup of hot tea might be nice—just something else to do for a moment and then leave undone. His work, papers mostly, printouts of some new reports as well as year-end and first-quarter figures, remained on the table, untouched and in two neat piles. The corners of the pages were flush with the corner of the table.

He placed a phone call to his friend and talked to her for a while, but she soon became too sleepy to speak. I'm fading, she said.

Come on, stay up, he said.

I'm fading fast.

Will you please stay up?

I have to get up early, she said.

How early? he asked. He thought if he could lure his friend into saying how early she needed to be awake, he could then lead her to explain what she planned to do so early, anyway, where she needed to be, and so forth. In this way, a single question opened entire fields of previously unexplored conversation. The fields were green. The grass was tall, up to his waist in places. Insects flung themselves into the air in high arcs. He wanted to be there, in those fields. He wanted to talk to someone.

I have to go, his friend said.

Really?

Really.

He placed the phone back in its cradle and looked at the clock. It was, he was relieved to see, fifteen minutes to the hour. In fifteen minutes, give or take, his girlfriend would return home. He was glad. He was, he thought, happy even.

The argument started an hour and fifteen minutes later. It wasn't the time, he took pains to point out, though he wasn't sure he believed that even as he heard himself say it. It wasn't that she had arrived home later than she guessed she'd probably be, or that he had worried, picturing various crimes, each violent to various degrees and each never to be solved, involving a parking lot, deserted save for her car, her, and a rotating cast of unsavory people, all men and most with beards, and most of them wearing hats the likes of which he'd never seen and so possessed no names for. It wasn't that, he said.

Well, she said, what is it?

I don't know, he said. He said I don't know the way many people say um or uh. It was a series of sounds, noise, really, to give him a chance to think. When he said he didn't know, usually he knew and was just looking for words.

She waited, saying nothing.

Finally, he said, It's just that you didn't seem at all bothered by the time, and I guess I was bothered, and so I started to think, I don't know, maybe I shouldn't have been so bothered, maybe I shouldn't have cared, because it's awful, you know, being the only person who cares.

That's ridiculous, she said. You're not the only person who cares.

That's how it looks from where I'm sitting, he said. He was lying on the bed, on his side of the bed, and she was lying beside him on hers. They were lying straight, like corpses in coffins, their arms at their sides. They addressed themselves to the ceiling, talking to beams. Occasionally she looked over at him, but then looked away.

Christ, she said.

Like this the argument wore on.

At some point he tried to remember what the argument was about, even, but failed. Was it about something? He didn't know. He really didn't know. Were there principles at stake? Probably not. Principles were never at stake when he believed them to be at stake. Then, did the argument have a cause? Or was it like a war, with subtleties so many and knotted as to occupy historians for years in the unraveling?

He remembered the fields of unexplored conversation, with the waist-high grass and the chittering insects, and again, as before, he wanted to be there. He wanted to talk to someone. He turned his head to look at his girlfriend. She was staring up at the ceiling until she heard him turn. She looked out the corners of her eyes and then turned her head partway toward him. A smile appeared on her face and then was gone, so quickly that the movement might have been involuntary, a twitch, a minute electrical current rushing beneath her skin.

You'll never believe what happened tonight, she said.

What's that?

Dorie got engaged.

Who?

Dorie, my friend, the woman I met up with tonight.

Oh, he said, really? He didn't think he knew Dorie. Maybe he had met her one time, somewhere. He wasn't sure.

She got engaged to this guy she met in September.

It was early November and just beginning to get cold. Sweater weather. He did the math, which was simple. Wow, he said.

That's not the least of it, she said. They got engaged on their first date. They went out to eat, Chinese, I think. He asked her out, and then, in the middle of dinner, he was like, Look, I don't know you all that well, but I feel like I know you well enough, and I know I want to keep getting to know you, so will you marry me?

Wow, he said. He didn't know what else to say. What does one say? He looked up at the ceiling. Wow, he said.

They don't have a ring, she said. A lot of people think it's a pretend engagement, because she doesn't have a ring, but they're getting one. They went to the jeweler the day after they got engaged and picked one out and ordered it. The ring's supposed to come in next week.

Wow, he said. He had wanted to talk but instead found himself speechless and not a little annoyed. All night, while he waited, he had wanted nothing more than to lie in bed and talk, but now that they were talking, he found that what he wanted was somewhat more specific: he didn't want to talk about this couple. His interest in the lives of this couple he didn't know—a couple he had never met or even laid eyes on—was waning. His girlfriend didn't really know them either. That was the truth of the matter. The woman, Dorie, was a friend of a friend. Still, he tried not to be judgmental— he tried hard—but he thought the couple silly, almost childlike, and ridiculous. They were a mockery of a couple. They were playing a game and playing it well, he supposed, seriously even, the way children do, their faces intent, their minds tightened fists, until, like

6

children, they lost interest, dropped everything, and moved on, to play seriously at something else.

They haven't been out again since they got engaged, his girlfriend said. I guess he doesn't like to go out or something.

Sounds charming.

He eats the same thing for dinner every night.

Wow, he said.

He's very into regularity, she said. He likes to have a routine.

He rubbed his eyes and covered his face with his hands. What does he eat, anyway? He wasn't sure he wanted to know the answer, but curiosity compelled him to ask.

Steak and steamed spinach.

Jesus, he eats steak every night?

He cooks the same meal for her. She eats it, too.

She eats the same thing every night?

She says she likes how it tastes.

I'm sorry, he said, but this sounds so ridiculous. They sound ridiculous.

When the ring comes in, they want to have some people over, she said. To celebrate.

Wonder what they'll serve at the party.

She looked at him. They want us to come over.

He put his hands behind his head and looked up at the ceiling. For a long while, he couldn't say anything.

What are you thinking? she asked.

I don't know, he said.

She looked up at the ceiling with him.

I'm just, he said, having a hard time caring about this couple. I know how that sounds. I know that's a harsh thing to say, but I feel like I could have an easier time caring about a couple of towheaded kids on some awful sitcom.

7

She didn't say anything. He went on.

They just sound so silly, he said. I just imagine celebrating with them, and what I picture is a bunch of people sitting on the floor, around a coffee table, sipping out of tiny toy teacups, or drinking grape juice out of wine goblets, and proposing toasts to the couple of the hour while trying to keep a straight face. It all just sounds like a big game of pretend, and it's their game of pretend, you know, and now they're asking other people to play with them, because the more people they get to come over and play, the realer the whole big, stupid game will appear.

His girlfriend provided further salient details about the woman (mother married young, father not alive, no previous serious relationship, had been dating someone else when her husband-to-be proposed). The man was a Mormon, and not much else was known. As she talked, he felt himself drowning in the trivia of strangers' lives. The more he thought of going to this couple's party, the more upset he grew. It would be a celebration of silliness—how could it not?—and he didn't want to play a part. He tried to find some way— some nice way—to say, Enough, please, no more, let's not talk about this ridiculous couple any longer, but for whatever reason, he could not. He wanted instead to talk about the two of them. They had just been arguing, after all. He wanted to finish that. He wanted to make good and make nice, smooth and pat. He wanted to say, Can't we talk about us, please?

Instead he said, Baby, I don't care. I already said I don't care. I just can't care about them. I don't know them. You don't know them. By the sound of things, they don't even know each other.

His girlfriend blinked, and her expression cooled.

You should care, she said. At the very least you should try to care, because this is something that happened to me tonight, and I'm telling you about it, because it disturbed me, because I think

8

it's strange for two people to get engaged on their first date and then spend the rest of their lives eating the same meal, because I just don't understand people, but I want to understand them, because otherwise I start to think that I'm the strange one. I came home and just wanted to lie down with you and talk to you and tell you what happened, because presumably you care about that.

He thought it wise not to continue the argument. He thought to stop it somehow. He thought to begin by easing off the couple, overlooking their ridiculousness, however galling he still found it, and letting it go. He wanted to say, Of course I care about you. He wanted to slip his arm underneath her and hold her to him and, perhaps, stroke the back of her head and rub her neck and say, Of course, of course, of course.

Why then he said what he said, propelling the argument forward even faster than before, will always remain a bit of a mystery to him. In any event, he said, Of course I care about you, which is exactly what he wanted to say, but he made the word care sound weak and sugary, and let it drip with false sentiment, and he pronounced it exactly as she pronounced it, a bit plaintively and with some urgency, mimicking her.

She hated when he mimicked her. She had told him, moreover, that she hated it, she had told him often, in fact, not to mimic her, but still, when they argued, he fell back with unfortunate frequency on the hopeless strategy of insincere imitation. He did not know why—he really did not know—except that he had always turned to mimicry, as long as he could remember, which, no, is not a good excuse, and perhaps not even a hollow rationalization, but rather a sad admission that mimicry had become, over time and with not a little practice, a habit of his being. Turning his back to his girl-friend when they were arguing was another habit of his being, as was shutting his eyes when confused or overwhelmed or cornered, rhetorically. Pulling the sheets and blanket over his chin and up to his mouth was a fourth habit. He surrendered himself to all these habits. He let them take over his person, giving into them with equal parts reluctance and comfort. He held the sheets and blankets to his mouth, muffling himself. He smelled the sheets and caught the perfume from the laundry detergent. He inhaled deeply, and the force of his breath drew the fabric into his mouth. The sheets smelled like futuristic lemons. He didn't say anything. At that moment, he didn't know what to say. He tasted the detergent and sucked lightly on the fabric and, for some time, he did not move.

PARABLE OF THE FEVER

ONE DAY and then another and still the fever has not broken. She is sick and doesn't know what to do. He is well and doesn't know what to do either. Nobody knows when the fever will break.

He looks at her and thinks, There's a hostile thing inside her, and I'd like to remove it, just pull it out somehow. He has these ideas that go nowhere, bold declarations to disguise his helplessness. He gets frustrated, and then he gets angry. What is to be done here? And what can he do for her, except wait?

He takes her temperature every hour, though she protests and would prefer if he just felt her forehead and sat beside her, holding her hand for a few minutes. The results are discouraging. Your temperature's gone down one-tenth of one degree, he tells her. He squints when he reads the mercury because he believes that will make his work more precise. In his mind, more precise is still closely related to more encouraging.

BESIDE MEDICINE and the counsel of doctors, folk remedies are a thin hope at best. He recommends she take a hot shower followed by a cold bath. He read that somewhere, he thinks. Later, he dampens a towel with cool water—cool, not cold—and places it on her forehead. Others suggest drinking a cup of tea with honey. Still others advise sipping from a glass of flat soda. Then a cold shower followed by no bath. At night, when she can't sleep, he wakes up with her, and they go to the kitchen. He runs the water until it's hot. Put your head into the steam, he says. He gets a towel and drapes it over her head, forming a tent. Does that feel okay? he says. He can't hear her. He puts his hands on her back and feels her breathe. He rubs her shoulders. After a few minutes, he realizes she's crying softly. He removes the towel and turns off the water. Maybe that's enough, he says. Her face is red, and her eyes are running. She rubs at her nose and says, Okay. Her hair has gone a little frizzy. It's kind of cute, he thinks. He just loves her so.

Folk remedies are like a cardboard box large enough to contain him and her and a few significant possessions. In the box, the fever swirls around them. As the fever passes by her, it fills her chest. It feels weird, but it feels like something she knows, too. She compares it to unspun cotton. Then she thinks, Cotton nested with weevils. The fever, meanwhile, continues to swirl; it fills her chest and then it passes on, leaving her depleted. Soon enough, this cycle leads to bankruptcy. She simply has nothing left for the fever to take.

The fever keeps a ledger of her debts. Owed, it writes at the top. It clucks its tongue as it calculates the total. This isn't looking good at all, the fever says. Then it gets back to swirling around them.

The fever stops for no one. It eyes her belongings. Then it lights on a few significant objects: a family picture from 1974, a favorite sweater, a trusty television. This will be mine, the fever says.

WHEN WILL THIS fever break?

They have no idea. They wish they knew.

I do know, or at least I have a good idea. I wish, though, I were like them, unsure. Knowledge is a kind of burden, like luggage. I know the fever will continue for a week more without breaking. At that time, their roles will reverse, and then he will have the fever.

They talk about the effectiveness of medicines and the merits of various active ingredients. She asks him, What do we do if this thing persists? He picks up a bottle of medicine and starts to read the label, looking for guidance.

I don't know, he says. This one just says don't take for more than ten days without consulting a physician.

They all say that, she says. They have to say that. It's the law or something.

Well, I'm just telling you what it says, he says.

She asks him to draw the curtains. I think I should rest, she says. Will you lie down with me?

He hesitates, not moving.

Please, she says.

He gets into bed beside her. All right, he says.

Under the blanket, she finds his hand and holds it. You feel nice, she says.

He squeezes her hand gently, just once, as if to say he's here, for her, even though the thing is, he doesn't really want to lie down. He has things to do, things he could be doing. Like reading. He has a lot of reading to do. And the truth is, he's tired of her being sick. He knows how terrible it is to think that, but he's tired.

After a few minutes, he slips his hand out from under hers and sits up in bed. Her breathing is raspy and full and deep. She doesn't move. I'll be back, he says. He whispers it so quietly he might be speaking to himself. He opens the door and is about to leave when she asks him where he's going. She sounds awake, alert.

I was just going to read, he says. It's too dark in here.

She rolls onto her side. I wish you'd just stay with me, she says. Just for a few minutes.

I can't lie in bed in the dark, he says. I'm sorry, but it makes me

13

crazy. He closes the door behind him and walks out into the light. He feels free. He actually thinks that. Finally, I'm free.

WHEN SHE AWAKES, it's already dark. She calls to him, and he goes to her at once. Hey, he says. Do you feel any better? He sits down on the edge of the bed and puts a hand on her shoulder. He's gentle. He wants to make up for before, if he needs to make up for before. She's so warm, he thinks.

She's not sure she's any better. Maybe a little, she says. I don't know.

You slept for three hours, almost, he tells her. I was starting to think maybe I should wake you up, to see if you want dinner. Do you want dinner?

She's not sure. What do we have? she says.

He doesn't know. He hasn't checked or, really, given it any thought. What do you want? he says. I'll get you whatever you want.

She says nothing sounds good to her.

You should eat, though, he says.

I know, she says, but nothing sounds good right now.

He tries her with a few suggestions, and she considers them, she does, but she's just not sure. If you make something, she says, I'll eat it. She holds his hand and pulls it toward her, to her face. I'm sorry, she says.

It's okay, he says. I'll get you better.

She nods. He feels her breath on his hand. You smell good, she says. She's said this before, at times, and he always thinks it's funny.

What do I smell like? he says.

Like you. It's nice.

Are you sure nothing sounds good to you? he says.

I can't think of anything.

All right, he says. He stands in the dark, looking around the room at the vague shapes of their things, at the bulk of their dresser and the outline of an old chair piled with clothes that need folding. I guess I'll go to the store then, he says, and get something. Something, in his mouth, sounds like an impossible request, as if she asked him to bring her the snow-covered top of her favorite mountain.

Before he leaves, she asks him for a glass of water. When he brings it to her, she says thank you. Something about how she says it makes it seem full of meaning, like she's thanking him for more than water.

It's okay, he says. Just try to rest. She nods and closes her eyes, and he thinks maybe she'll sleep again and maybe that's for the best.

HE WANDERS UP and down the aisles, trying to shop for his girlfriend. What would she like? What would he like for that matter, if he were her and sick? He's not sure. He has no mind for food. He knows some food is better than other food—better tasting and better for you—but none of it seems that much better, really, to him. The fact is he could eat anything, pretty much, at any meal, and that would be just fine. He doesn't get cravings like some people do. He doesn't even understand them. Sometimes she tells him, I could really go for Thai tonight. The very idea is foreign to him. How does she know she could go for Thai? How can she tell? She might as well have said I could really use a pet bird right about now.

He picks out ingredients for a salad but then puts them all back. Then he finds some pasta and stuff to make a nice red sauce. Nothing fancy, no cream or anything. He gets some fizzy water, for her stomach, if she needs that, and some of this juice she loves that comes in a little bottle shaped like a bud vase. Then he passes by the floral department and, on an impulse, selects a bouquet of mixed flowers. Something pretty, hc thinks. The bouquet is large, and the flowers have long stems. Holding them in front of him, cradled in his arm, he feels like he just won a beauty pageant.

At the checkout, the cashier wants to chat. She picks up the little bottle of juice and says, Now this is cute. She shows it to him, as if he has never seen it before. Then she turns to the woman working at the next register over. Look how cute this is, she says. She holds it up for all to see. They both agree it's one cute bottle of juice.

My girlfriend likes them, he says. He doesn't know why he says anything. It'll only encourage her.

The cashier scans the juice. Girlfriend's got expensive taste, she says. Mercy. She turns the register's screen so he can read it. Is that the right price? she says.

He says he thinks it is.

Really?

Yes, he says. Really.

The cashier shakes her head. Is it real good or something? she says.

It's pretty good, he says.

Ought to be better than pretty good, she says. Juice that expensive would have to make me smarter or something.

The cashier continues scanning his items. Pasta tonight? she asks.

What's that? he says. He'd just been spacing, thinking about his girlfriend, if he had everything he needed.

Are you making pasta tonight? the cashier says. She speaks a little more slowly, for his benefit.

Yeah, he says.

You forgot garlic, the cashier says.

He thinks for a second. We have garlic at home, he says. We should, anyway.

All right, the cashier says. She puts her hands up. I'm only just trying to help.

The flowers still lie at the end of the conveyor belt. He wants to indicate them, to move this along and get home, but he doesn't want to be rude.

The cashier turns on the conveyor belt, and the flowers move toward her, summoned. I'm not going to forget your flowers, she says.

Thank you, he says.

Man's got to have his flowers, she says.

He nods, awaiting a total and that is all.

You in the doghouse or something? she says.

What? he asks. No, I'm—

The cashier laughs. She bends over double, just cackling away. People waiting at other registers nearby look over their way, to see what's so funny. They want in, too, to be part of the fun. The cashier shakes her head and tries to compose herself. I'm just messing with you, she says. You should have seen your face, though. Small tears form at the corners of her eyes.

My girlfriend's sick, he says. He just wants to leave. He has his wallet out and he wants to leave.

Well, the cashier says, I wish my boyfriend got me flowers when I was sick of him.

My girlfriend's really sick, he says. She has a high fever.

The cashier nods, as if fever's exactly what she's talking about. Sick is sick, she says.

What's that supposed to mean? he says.

I just mean maybe you made her sick, the cashier says. People

17

do do that sometimes, you know. Maybe they don't mean to, but it happens. I've read about it in books.

I'm not sure that's what's going on here, he says. He fishes some money out of his wallet and cranes his neck to look at the register's screen. The total has to be there somewhere.

The cashier taps a couple of keys on the register and then presents him with his total. You ever hear somebody say you make me sick? she asks.

He shakes his head. That's something else, he says. I know what you're saying, but that's something else.

The cashier tells him she hopes he has a good night.

In the parking lot, he stands by his car and looks back at the store, glaring at the front of the building. Fucking cow, he thinks. Fucking cashier cow. He puts his groceries in the car and then stands there, listening. He thinks maybe he should do something, but he doesn't know what. Maybe he could speak to some assistant manager. He's not sure. The lights overhead hum and cast an evil yellow glow over the entire lot. The air is full of little insects. They're all over. He just notices them, swarming, but they've always been there. They surround his head and body, like fuzz or an extra layer of himself. When he moves, they move with him. He swats at them, and for a second they float away, out of sight, but then they return, drifting back, if anything, in thicker numbers. He doesn't know what they are. They don't seem to bite. They just annoy. They make a sound, high-pitched, like the whine of a tiny motor. He flails his arms around his head and then jumps into the car. The insects, some of them, get inside before he can close the door, and so he sits there, swatting at them wildly, trying to kill them all. They're everywhere, though.

PRAYER FOR THE BABY, STILL EXPECTED

THE YOUNG COUPLE did not tell their friends they were expecting a baby until they were completely sure. They had had several false alarms before and one miscarriage. They had endured more misfortune than most young couples and so knew it was best for all concerned if they waited.

Two months later the doctor told the couple they had a baby and that the baby appeared healthy. All systems, he said, were go.

That night, the couple took their friends out to eat. They went to a little Thai place they all liked, and as the husband passed his wife the red curry dish, and the wife passed her friend the Thai basil dish, the husband looked from one friend to the other and said, We have a little bit of news.

The woman friend looked up from her plate. She heard something in his voice, a catch or a certain tone, and expected the worst. She almost always expected the worst. The man friend waited, leaning toward good news because who, after all, invites friends out for anything other than good news?

The wife looked at her husband and then back at her friends and said, I'm pregnant.

The husband put his arm around his wife's shoulders and squeezed. We're having a baby, he said.

The friends expressed their congratulations and wonder. How miraculous it was, they said, and how lucky the couple was. They would make the perfect parents. There was some mention of the couple's earlier misfortunes, but only to say, thank god, that's passed, thank god. The dinner seemed to finish itself.

Not long after, the couple decided the best way to prepare for the new baby was to practice being parents, to pretend as if the baby had already arrived and they had to care for it.

The young couple went to elaborate lengths. They bought a stroller, a cradle, and a car seat. They bought baby clothes and baby toys. The husband made a baby out of a throw pillow, shaping it into a kind of lumpy body. The wife fashioned a face for their baby and then took some of her hair, a lock or two only, really, and glued it to the fabric. Though the pillow was green, almost silvery, like the underside of certain leaves, when they were done, it did look, they had to admit, more or less like a baby.

That night, the young couple met their friends again for dinner at the little Thai place. The girlfriend gave the wife a big hug and then held her at arm's length, just looking at her, as if she were contemplating a purchase. The wife wasn't really showing yet, the girlfriend thought. At least not that she could tell. You look so beautiful, the girlfriend said. You know that, right? She gave the wife another hug.

The young couple had brought their baby with them and, while they waited for the food to arrive, the wife took the baby out of its special seat and passed the baby to her husband.

The husband said, It's a bit cold in here. He rooted through their baby-supply bag and found a blanket. When the baby was snugly wrapped, he passed the bundle to the woman friend. She looked at the throw pillow, fixed the baby's eyes with her eyes, and said, What a beautiful baby. What a beautiful baby. Then she handed the bundle to the man friend.

The man friend agreed. It is beautiful. He looked at the young couple, worried he may have offended them. But they just smiled to see him with their dear baby.

After dinner arrived, the young couple attended to the baby

first. They interrupted their friends to say the baby was crying, the baby needed feeding, the baby needed changing, or the like. The baby was always either too hot or too cold. The baby was tired and needed to be rocked gently, slowly, or the baby was cranky and crying and so needed to be entertained. The husband lifted the baby to the ceiling and then pulled the baby close. He made motorboat sounds and then he made bubble-blowing sounds. The whole restaurant turned to watch the spectacle of a man playing with a throw pillow wrapped up in a blanket.

Later that night, the man friend and the woman friend were at home, at her apartment, getting ready for bed. The woman stood in the bathroom, looking at herself in the mirror. The man sat on the edge of the bed and looked at his feet. He massaged the tops of his thighs and then rested his hands on his knees. They were alone, finally. They took off their clothes and lay down, and the man sighed.

What is it, darling? the woman asked.

The man was looking at the ceiling, at a hole that he sometimes imagined, he didn't know why, could house a tiny camera. I don't know, he said. I don't know.

When the man said he didn't know, he usually did, in fact, know but was trying to put whatever it was into words that wouldn't come out all wrong. The woman moved her hand across the man's chest and waited a moment.

So, the man said, what did you think of that baby?

They're just trying, the woman said.

It's a pillow, the man said. I mean, I'm sorry for stating the obvious, but it's just a pillow.

They're trying their best, the woman said.

You're a lot more generous than I am, the man said. I looked at that pillow and I was like, it's a goddamn pillow.

21

Right, the woman said.

I mean, it's green.

I know, the woman said.

The man turned to face the woman. And you, he said, You deserve the Academy Award for that what a beautiful baby business. The man pulled the pillow from under his head, clutched it to his chest, and started to make cooing sounds. Jesus, he said. What a beautiful baby, he said. That was really great.

The woman didn't say anything.

It was green, the man said.

The woman said, I know it wasn't a baby, but nevertheless, I believed it was.

The man said, I knew it was a green pillow and nevertheless believed it to be a green fucking pillow.

I'm just worried, the woman said.

You mean if they accidentally kill their pillow? the man said.

The woman ignored him. He could be his most insensitive when he thought he was being funny, on some kind of roll. I'm worried, she said, about what will happen if they don't have the baby.

The man put his pillow back into place and petted the back of the woman's head. Okay, he said.

They're putting everything into this, the woman said. I mean, everything.

I know, the man said, though he really only half knew and was half waiting to hear the rest.

I worry about what'll happen if the baby doesn't come along to replace the pillow.

The pillow will just go back to being a pillow, probably, the man said. Right? Don't you think?

Maybe the pillow will stay a baby, the woman said.

The couple shifted and stirred under the cover of the sheets. The man was looking at the ceiling again. The woman had her head in the crook of his arm.

Why green? the man said. You have to ask yourself, Why green?

The woman turned away, onto her side. She could usually get to sleep this way.

The man said, Green is just inviting something bad to happen, right?

The woman pulled the sheets around her and drew her legs up. The pillow could just stay a baby, she said.

PARABLE OF
THE NEXT MOST BEAUTIFUL THING

THE FIRST most beautiful thing was a line of my boot prints in the snow. The line went from my front door straight across the field to the store where Grubbs sold me the food I needed.

The first most beautiful thing lasted for two weeks, which is when I grew bored with looking at it. To view the most beautiful thing, I decided, is to consume it, eating it whole, chewing it up fast and smacking my lips. But supping heartily on the most beautiful thing each and every day can reduce even a delicacy to a pot full of potatoes boiled too long. I had become dissatisfied with my creation. I resented its simplicity.

The next time I went to see Grubbs, I didn't take the shortest route. Sure, I had my critics. And yes, they weren't prepared to embrace my undertaking. My most vocal detractor was a man who lived halfway across the field, squatting with his family in a broken-down Airstream. No one knew how they got there, and no one asked. The man was forever stoking a fire and leaning over it, as if he were hiding the flames from enemies. His family kept well behind him. His children were thin and pasty creatures, but quite lively, like a long-haired little army. They enjoyed throwing rocks, and a couple of the older ones had arms on them. As I walked past, the man called out to me. Hey, boy, he said. I stopped to listen. The first most beautiful thing was far better than this. He swept his hands like whisk brooms, brushing dirt off something valuable.

That might be true, I said.

My walk to Grubbs and back took longer than usual, but when

working at the next most beautiful thing, such devotion was to be expected.

The second most beautiful thing did not last as long as the first. I was well into the afternoon and deep into a bag of mixed nuts when disappointment came over me. Such reckonings occur, in my experience, between the third and fourth hours, when it's too late to do anything differently with the day, but not so late that you don't have quite a few hours still to bitch and moan.

Evening came, though, and morning followed—and with it the third most beautiful thing.

The man was standing by his Airstream. An impressive fire came up to his chin. His children were stripping sticks of their leaves. His wife sat on the ground winding lengths of copper wire around a coffee can. These people were always getting up to something together. Several containers of soup were stacked close by, and a few cooking implements dangled from a chain strung between two pine trees.

The man called me over once more. Boy! he said. Hey, boy.

As I drew near, the wife and kids hustled indoors. I stopped just opposite the man, keeping the fire between us.

You suppose, he said, that the third time's the charm?

I don't know, I said. I don't like to make predictions.

The man shook his head and tossed some sticks at his fire. I feel sorry for you, he said.

This time I zigged where I zagged and zagged where I formerly zigged. I took running leaps to create the illusion of superhuman steps and, keeping my feet together, alternated this with short, quick, and halting hops in the snow.

Later, I prepared a bowl of chicken broth with a couple of crackers floating in it. As I sipped at my soup, I looked on the third most beautiful thing and declared it good.

I let my work stand unchanged for eight days, but then I could bear it no longer. That night I read from Charles Dickens, one of the fat novels. With the book weighing on my chest, I dreamed of a city populated by highly intelligent squirrels. For some reason I was there trying to obtain a special necklace. I went from store to store and block to block, looking for a jeweler, or else a squirrel who could direct me to one. When I awoke, it was early and still dark out. I felt like ass, like I hadn't even slept. I lay in bed and plotted what wild and as yet unseen fourth path I would step off that day.

The man warned me not to approach. He was waving his arms about in agitated semaphore. Boy! he said. You leave it be. You can only make this worse.

I stopped my cartwheels, which I was interspersing with a series of end-overs, and came up to where he stood.

This thing, he said, nodding toward my work-in-progress, it's got to seem artless. It should also appear unconscious and embody one of the forty-nine universal truths. It should be transparent yet muscular. Wise and forgiving. Above all, it should be humble. It should announce itself quietly as the leader of a nation of subtle things. I nodded, just so he knew I had heard him. Then he pointed to my forehead. That's sweat, he said. I ran my hand across my head. It was, in fact, sweat. Christ, he said, that's what I'm warning you about.

My trips to Grubbs were taking longer and making me increasingly tired. When I wasn't out stepping off the next most beautiful thing, I was indoors, in bed, recuperating with Dickens. I read a few pages each night and then fell asleep. I lost my place, but sometimes I could continue the story in my mind, just making it all up. I dreamed I wore metal shoes and had no hair. I dreamed of a town where the women set fire to themselves. I dreamed a band of those brilliant squirrels rescued me from certain death only to turn around and make me stand trial on some trumped-up

27

charges not even the squirrel lawyer appointed to represent me could explain.

I avoided the man as best I could, but he called out to me criticisms many and various. On the fifth day, he said, the god of gods brought forth all kinds of living creatures. Cattle just for starters, but also creeping things, flying things, and stuff with stripes. To say nothing of the first human beings. What will you do by comparison?

Stopping to argue would have interfered with my overall design. Besides, I had no good answer. What I did had, I thought, its merits and its failings. Still, I had some idea of what the man was getting at, and I envied him his confidence and his certainty. I envied, too, his family. They were a scruffy bunch, especially the children. I bet they had jokes between them that only they could understand. Anecdotes, too. None could ever mistake their love.

In the morning, I judged what I had done, and figured it good, or at least okay. As before, though, it didn't last. After less than a week, I found the fifth most beautiful thing wanting.

Evening came, and morning followed. Days of the week bled together into one longer day punctuated by several periods of hazy light, periods I mostly just slept through. In the afternoon, I ate a can of soup, whatever I had. I didn't care what flavor. I couldn't be bothered. Because what was taste, finally, except some dotty monarch sitting alone in his garden and addressing himself to the sun, telling it about how his majesty had decided he preferred the blue-green china to that inferior green-blue stuff?

Everything I ate came in packages or cans. They were easy to carry. I liked my food in small boxes decorated with pictures of what, in a perfect world, my meal might resemble. I guess I just liked seeing what I was shooting for. I ate what I ate. Then I went outside in the interest of beauty. Later, in the evenings, I read more Dickens. For a while there, I had a real routine going, a schedule to keep—every day a thing more beautiful—except I got tired, and I grew hungry. To create the next most beautiful thing, I had to travel farther out of the way. My trips to see Grubbs now ran upwards of five miles, counting the many circles I made. I also had to buy more food, because I was more active, I moved more. I was, in some sense, more productive. Beauty was limited by my stomach, which felt hunger, and by my feet, which felt soreness.

. Charles Dickens, you lived off your gut, did you not? Your paunch. Each of your books attached themselves to the inside of your stomach. They lined your intestines. Underneath a fold of tissue, there was *Nicholas Nickleby*. Around a turn in the small intestine, *Oliver Twist*. They fastened themselves there with metal teeth. Like lampreys, their bites left marks, little rings. Somehow, though, you had enough to sustain them, to sustain yourself, to continue. Most of the time, I didn't worry about how I would continue, or what I would do.

I packed a bag with some provisions and headed across the field toward the Airstream. It was late, and the night chilly, but the man was by his fire still, tending to it. He never slept.

Boy! he said. Is the next most beautiful thing going to begin in darkness?

I continued toward him. I wasn't up to anything fancy. I was just walking.

Style's a bit plain, the man said. Don't you think?

I just came to talk, I said.

The man looked doubtful. This part of some new act? he said.

I shook my head no.

Because you're not appropriating me, he said. I want no part of anything, you understand?

Like I said, I'm just here to talk.

The man sat down and then pointed at a patch of ground beside him. Talking, he said. Now why does that sound so dreary?

I'm not sure.

Well, when I get lonely, the man said, I like to burn stuff.

I took a couple of containers of soup out of my bag. You want any? I asked.

Depends, the man said. What do you got?

I picked up one of the containers and read the label. Beef leek, I said. I checked the other container. More beef leek, looks like. Sorry, I said.

The man thought for a moment. Beef leek's not terrible, he said.

He fetched us a pot and some utensils. The pot snapped into a wire contraption that kept it suspended over the flames at just the right height.

That's pretty ingenious, I said.

Fits all your traditional pot sizes, the man said. He showed me how it worked, how the wire collapsed around the pot, encircling it, somewhat like a fisherman's net and somewhat like a drawstring pouch.

I admired the contraption like a horse could be said to admire the car. Where did you get it? I said.

Invented it myself, the man said.

I was impressed, and I told him as much.

Despite what you may think, he said, it's not all pancakes and grab-ass over here.

When the soup was ready, I served some to the man and then ladled out a small bowl for me.

The man took a few sips and then considered them. Well, he said, it's not the absolute worst beef leek I've ever eaten.

I told the man then how I'd been doing some thinking.

That's your first mistake right there, he said.

I'm thinking, I said, that maybe the most recent beautiful thing should be the last most beautiful thing.

Oh, god, the man said. Please don't tell me you're switching to some other medium.

I'm thinking about quitting, I said. Or maybe just taking a little time off.

He brought the soup to his mouth and blew on it. Sabbatical might do you good, he said. New perspective, clarity, all that.

I just thought I should let you know, I said.

Well, I appreciate that, the man said. If you had stopped coming around, I would have wondered what happened. Like maybe you had died in bed or fallen into a snowdrift and frozen to death. I have what is called a catastrophic turn to my mind, he said. I dream of natural disasters.

If you guys ever disappeared, I said, I would wonder, too.

We're not going anywhere, the man said. This place is perfect.

Sitting next to the man, by his fire, I could grasp the appeal. The Airstream was like a shiny node in an intricate system of wire. The wires ran everywhere, crisscrossing overhead. More of his inventions, I supposed. Tools and various little boxes were lashed to rocks and the trunks of trees. It was as if the family feared their stuff might float away, so they bound everything to the surroundings in a hundred different ways. I liked the setup, and not just the jerry-rigging, but the odd logic that pulsed behind it.

Maybe I could stay with you guys? I said.

The man sat looking into the fire.

I could bring all my soups over, I said. And I could stay just for a few days. Or longer, if you wanted. I wouldn't be any drag on you.

My kids would stone you dead, the man said.

I laughed to think of it. Their rocks raining down, and me running about, dodging them, like in some game where I have extra lives.

You think I'm joking, the man said. My kids despise you.

But you could control them, I said. Couldn't you? In my mind, I had already moved in. I was part of the family. True, they had looked on me with suspicion, at least at first, but gradually, I won them over. I guess they got to where they appreciated my charms or whatever. The children played with me. Chase. Hide-and-seek. The classics. I was like their new uncle. I even let them do some rock throwing. I loved them all. And I helped out where I could, with the garbage or the teaching. I did whatever they needed. If we needed wire, I scavenged for it. I thought it could work, my plan. I knew it sounded a little crazy, but still I had this hope, however frail, and I just held on to it like a guy caught in a windstorm hanging onto his last possession.

It would never work, the man said.

Well, think it over, I said. I don't need to know right this second.

I'm telling you, the man said, it will not work.

The light of the fire flickered across his features, making his face into a leering mask.

I had a girlfriend once, the man said. She was my first real girlfriend, I guess you would say. Everything was fine between us, except I could not fall asleep with her. It didn't matter what I did. It didn't matter whether we lay down with me behind her, holding her, or if we tried it with her pressing up against me. Touching her, even if I was just putting my arms around her, got me too keyed up. I lay awake thinking—I don't remember exactly what I thought, but stuff ran through my mind, stupid stuff, stuff like, Look at me, touching my girlfriend, how very swell. It was maddening. I only wanted to relax. I wanted to drift off. Then I wanted to wake up beside her, in the morning, with some thin strip of sun squeezing through the blinds, and I wanted to say, Hey, darling, good morning, how are you feeling? All I had to do was fall asleep, but I couldn't do it. Can you see what I'm getting at here?

Not really, I said.

The man sighed and looked off, away from me. I'm just saying some things don't work out the way you want them to. In addition to that, it doesn't matter how much you want what you think you want. In the end, you just get what you get.

All right, I said. It was just a thought. It doesn't matter.

Look, you're tired, the man said. You should rest. Take that break or something.

I nodded. Sure, okay.

I know you, he said. You'll be right back at this. In no time.

PRAYER FOR AN ANSWER
WHEN AN ANSWER ELUDES

Dorie and her fiancé had invited another couple over for dinner and a small celebration. They were recently engaged.

From the living room, Dorie's friend called out, asking if she could be of some assistance. Her boyfriend ducked into the kitchen. Is there anything I can do, he said, to help out?

Dorie was standing by the stove, steaming spinach in a pot. I think I've got everything under control, she said. But thank you.

The boyfriend felt relieved. Recycling? he said. He held up a couple of empties. Dorie turned from the stovetop and pointed with her foot. Under the sink, she said.

The boyfriend dropped the bottles and headed outside, to the patio, to see how the fiancé was managing with the grill. All he could do, though, was hold the door as the fiancé came back inside, carrying a platter stacked high with meat. The boyfriend knew little about this couple. He knew they got engaged after one date, during their first date, actually, at some Chinese restaurant. It was as if the very idea of getting engaged had gone on sale, its price drastically reduced. Everyone was buying now. Besides that, his girlfriend had warned him that the man of the couple ate the same dinner every night.

Just please don't make a big deal out of it, she said. We could use more friends, okay?

The boyfriend thought they sounded like real prizes. At his most charitable, he figured they deserved each other. What he meant was nobody else deserved them.

Mmm, steaks, the woman said. She'd come around the corner to make sure she couldn't help.

Are steaks the chef's specialty? her boyfriend asked.

The fiancé stammered a bit, and his face turned a fierce red. I guess you could say that, he said.

The boyfriend clapped him on the shoulder. Well, that's just great, he said. I love a good steak.

His girlfriend put an enormous quantity of silverware into his hands, enough for a table of eight eating a meal of no fewer than four courses, and then piled a number of steak knives on top. He left the kitchen, burdened, and headed for the table. I look forward to giving that spinach a whirl, too, he said.

Dinner was ready. The woman looked around the table appreciatively. Her boyfriend, hungry and eager to eat, waited. Why are we here? he thought. Why did we come? He looked at his girlfriend and smiled. Dorie turned then to her fiancé and asked him if he would like to say his blessing. He nodded a bit, shyly, and made a small sound, like the peep of a baby animal. He reached for her hand and then for the boyfriend's hand. Then he bowed his head and spoke these words: Thanks to my grandmother, we are able to eat tonight this steak and this steamed spinach. Thank you, Grandmother. I love you, and I appreciate your continued guidance in this life I lead. With that, the fiancé raised his head, smiled to the woman and her boyfriend, and started the spinach on its way around the table.

That was a very interesting blessing, the boyfriend said. He accepted the bowl of spinach and reached to pick up a serving fork. Personally, he considered most meals pretty much complete without a blessing. Blessings exasperated him. Whenever he mimed prayer, faking the necessary solemnity, he had to fight hard not to roll his eyes. He always felt like, who were these people kidding? They spoke not a word of god (or whomever). They never went to church (or wherever), and yet here they were, blessing their food. It was just food, he thought, and it was getting colder by the self-regarding minute.

Sometimes, however, blessings made him cry. Not bawl, but tear up. A little. It was always a surprise, a shock really, to feel when he expected to feel nothing. All the figurative language of feeling pertained. He understood, for instance, what it meant to feel touched. And his heart, his heart was pulled out of place, turned by the words like a screw in a hole. On those occasions—they were rare—he liked the way people, a family, some friends, what have you, joined together. He liked the intensity of the moment, the concentration. Above all, he liked the quiet. He even liked holding hands, at least for a minute. It was as if he were walking through the woods and came upon a wild animal—a skittish fox, say, in a patch of moonlight, or a fawn tugging leaves from a bush, or a hummingbird flirting with a blossom. He stood near enough to that wild thing to recognize it as truly amazing, a mystery around which all life was arrayed. And he realized, not for the first time but the first time in a while, that he was there merely to spectate and, if he was lucky, happen occasionally upon the miraculous. Those blessings, though, were addressed to one of the world's major deities, not some guy's grandmother.

His grandmother was so important to him growing up, Dorie said. She stroked her fiancé's neck. She was like this role model for him and his younger brother.

That right? the boyfriend said. Such work, pretending to care. He was struggling to lift an object larger than himself.

His parents, Dorie said, were rather severe people, isn't that right, honey?

The fiancé nodded and watched the platter of steaks head toward him, going from the woman to Dorie.

His parents were Mormons through and through, Dorie said. They were also real disciplinarians, especially when it came to raising kids. They punished the children harshly, beating them sometimes with the belt and making them kneel on the floor. She turned to her fiancé. You should tell this, she said.

The fiancé, who had not spoken since his blessing, reached for his water and took a sip. The ice clinked pleasantly against the glass. He needed a drink, but he also just wanted some business to do with his hands and mouth. Anything other than talking. Please, he said. He looked to Dorie. You tell it. You tell it better anyway.

Dorie turned back to the woman and her boyfriend. The woman nodded for her to continue, and her boyfriend motioned vaguely with the end of his fork as he chewed. Well, basically, she said, his parents had this thing where they always insisted that the two boys finish their dinner. They made them sit at the table for hours, until they ate every bite. Sometimes, their mother cleared the table and cleaned up in the kitchen, and still they sat. She would take out the garbage and turn off the lights and only then, finally, did she relent. After consulting with her husband, she excused the boys from the table and sent them to their room, where they knelt at the foot of their bunk bed until told to wash up and get to sleep.

Dorie sipped her wine, and the boyfriend took the opportunity to compliment the fiancé on the steak. Mine is done to perfection, he said.

Yes, the woman said, it's really quite good.

The fiancé blushed again, as if noticing that he sat before them naked. Thank you, he said. I'm so glad you like it.

Anyway, Dorie said, one day, the boys' grandmother visited. Their parents were out of town—they had to go out of town for something, they traveled every now and then—so their grandmother came to stay with them, to take care of them. She had heard from the parents that the children were picky eaters, and so as soon as the parents were gone, she announced her plans to fix a meal especially for them.

She said it would be a special feast, the fiancé added. She used those words, special feast. He spoke as if he were young again, as if the years that had passed fell away and left him a boy whose bunk bed served as a ship lost at sea or a fort under attack by minions.

Anyway, that special feast, Dorie said, is the one you're enjoying now. The woman looked up from her plate, and her boyfriend did his best to appear honored, touched, without overdoing it and turning everything mawkish.

The fiancé said, Tell them about how she prepared it. They'll like that.

Dorie said, The boys' grandmother made a big production. It really was a feast by the sound of things. She turned on the classical music station and sang along with the operas.

She had this great, big, booming voice, the fiancé said. He clutched at his heart with both his hands and then slowly extended one arm until it was fully outstretched and his palm was open, reaching to catch something valuable as it fell from the sky. The boyfriend half expected the fiancé to give a demonstration and sing for them right there. Instead, he dropped his hands into his lap. No illusion could suffice. When my grandmother sang, he said, she just filled up the room.

She sang all the while she cooked, Dorie said, and when dinner was almost ready, she set the table with fancy china and silver and she lit candles, and they ate only by the candlelight, right, honey?

The fiancé nodded. I seem to have forgotten the candles tonight, he said.

It's beautiful exactly how it is, the woman said.

It's perfect, her boyfriend said. He looked at the fiancé and tried to express concern and then empathy and then concern again, but he felt, as he often did, that his face was a slippery thing, sliding out from under his control.

Well, Dorie said, of course the boys ate everything. And they finished their food without any duress. Dorie asked for more spinach, and the boyfriend passed the bowl to her. The next night, Dorie said, the boys and their grandmother had the same thing for dinner. Same with the night after that.

Big production every night? the boyfriend asked.

The fiancé nodded.

She put on the same show for her grandsons night after night, Dorie said. For the whole week their parents were gone.

That's something, the boyfriend said.

What happened when your parents got back? the woman asked.

When my parents got back, the fiancé said, they— As he spoke, he looked down at his plate and carefully aligned his fork next to his knife. The table was a complex machine that operated only when all the individual parts were in their proper positions.

I don't want to pry, the woman said.

No, no, the fiancé said. I was only thinking.

It's okay, the woman said. I'm sorry I asked. Really. I can see now I shouldn't have asked.

Please, the fiancé said. He held up his hands as if he were stopping traffic. I don't mind, he said. My parents just didn't appreciate what my grandmother had done. She told them of her success in getting us to eat. She told them all about the opera music and the candlelight and the steaks and about how we ate every bite. My brother and I crouched by the door to the den, and we listened. Their reaction was—my parents' reaction was just, you know, You shouldn't spoil our children like that, or whatever. I can't remember the exact words. Then my father told her—this was his mom, mind

40

you—that he too would like to eat steak every day, but the fact of the matter was, he couldn't afford it. Well, my brother and I, we ran back to our bedroom. We were supposed to be asleep.

Steak *is* expensive, the boyfriend said. I mean, you do have yourself an expensive habit here.

The fiancé looked as if he'd been struck across the face. He opened his mouth to speak, but then picked up his glass and studied the ice floating in the water. It was nearly melted. The cubes looked like jumbled-up geometry problems. They were just an idea now of something slightly colder.

I'm not defending the guy, the boyfriend said. I'm just talking about the cost. How it would add up.

We never had the steaks again, the fiancé said. They never fixed them for us. He looked at his plate, searching for something mixed in with the juice from the steak and the water from the spinach. And they must have told my grandmother not to fix us that special feast anymore too, because when she came back, we had just regular meals with her, with, you know, no frills.

Dorie touched her fiancé's arm and said, Things just went back to exactly how they were before, in terms of the boys having to sit at the table until excused and kneel on the floor for their punishment.

I can see why you'd resent your parents, the woman said.

The fiancé said, actually, he didn't resent them any longer. At the time, he said, but not now.

It was a long time ago, Dorie added.

My parents did their best, the fiancé said. His estimation hung there, obviously incomplete. It was only half of what he believed, true in part. It wanted modification, anger to undo it, a simple but. He pushed his knife ever so slightly away from him. Then he pinched his fork by the neck and realigned it again with the knife. What are you going to do? he said. He had thought of many less generic things to say. Some thoughts came to him with stingers and barbs attached, or with a sudden jolt, as if a swarm of eels had brushed by him. He could be childish too, petulant even. In anger, he uttered familiar swear words in novel combinations. He had spent years honing the sharp edges of his favorite curses. My parents were limited people, he said. They lived in a cozy town. As they grew older, they hardly ever left their house. They were these tiny jeweled figurines, twirling and dancing and going around and around inside a padded music box. And yet they couldn't have been happier.

The boyfriend thought this sounded like resentment by another, more sophisticated name, to him at least. But what did he know?

Dorie said, His parents are no longer with us.

My mother died, the fiancé said, and then my father died. It was a few months later, but close enough so that one seemed to cause the other. My father stopped cutting his fingernails. And then he left the refrigerator open for probably two weeks. Then he stopped opening his mail. Stacks of bills and catalogs and cards and letters piled up behind the door. When I visited, I had to shove it open, like you would if there was a snowdrift. My father just didn't care. It was sad. I didn't want to feel sad, but I did.

The boyfriend excused himself and went to find the bathroom. In the hallway, Dorie and her fiancé had hung a series of photographs, some framed snapshots and Polaroids, some more formal, professional portraits, all of the same woman, the grandmother, presumably, taken at different times in her life and in different places. The hallway was lined with the photographs, on both sides. The boyfriend bent to peer more closely at a picture. In it, the grandmother wore an overcoat, buttoned to her neck, and a clever hat with a flower on the front. She had on gloves and polished, pointy shoes. Her ankles were thick and sturdy. Maybe, the boyfriend thought, this photo was taken when she visited the boys and made them that feast. She looked about the right age. The woman was gripping her handbag in front of her and held it away from her body a bit, as if she preferred the handbag to be photographed instead. He tried to imagine what the grandmother was like. How had she spoken to the boys? And how had she then talked to their parents? Was she angry in her righteousness, or beyond calm? Had she been a talented cook? Or was she only better by comparison? Was she just welcome relief, a day in the high eighties to follow a week of unrelenting heat? The boyfriend tried to picture her visits. He pictured himself refusing to eat. He had never much liked cauli-flower and pork chops, or canned pears and mashed potatoes. And then he pictured himself kneeling before his bed, beside the brother he did not have.

His childhood had been decent, if not happy. He'd never known his grandparents, but he had no complaints overall. If anything, he had tormented others. In school, in the sixth grade, he and his friends surrounded a boy, this small kid, black, kind of underde-veloped looking, and punched him, repeatedly, in the stomach. He can't remember why, or what the pretense was, if they ever even had one. Had the kid done or said something to a friend of theirs?

This was in the morning, before class. It was first period, life science. The teacher stood in the hall, chatting with the other teach-ers, the way she always did. Why does he recall that it was a science class but not what they told themselves they were doing? He can picture charts and diagrams on the walls, their homework, stacked and graded, a poster of mollusks, a cutaway view of the human body, and, beside the teacher's desk, a skeleton on wheels. The guys pushed the kid into a corner, the corner farthest from the door, and hit him. They took turns. He, the boyfriend, was last to go. His was a cowardly punch, really. They'd all turned to walk away, to go to their desks and sit up straight and appear ready to learn, when he

43

decided he wanted his shot. It was ugly, thuggish, unforgivable. He still thought about it from time to time. Had something come over him, or was there, in fact, something inside him that was revealed? And that kid, did he remember what they had done? Did he think about it still?

Sympathy—sympathy of the deepest, most honest sort—required that the boyfriend wrestle with such questions. Yet however mightily he struggled, and he did struggle, he emerged with provisional answers and little else. Presuming and supposing only got him so far, so he had to fashion his best guesses at how it was, being someone else, from his experiences, twisting off their particulars and snipping them from their context, forcing them to fit the new circumstances. What was the grandmother like? When she sang, how did she sound? Was her voice soft? Did it carry through the house? Did it fill the boys with a feeling they learned later to call joy? The boyfriend could run for years toward these questions, which, like mountains, only seemed to recede. But he had to run. He had to pursue them. A person simply had to run, and had to keep running.

After dinner was done and drinks were drunk, after they had talked into the night and then said their good-byes and made frequent, albeit ambiguous promises to get together real soon and, you know, do something or hang out or something, the woman and her boyfriend relaxed on their couch in front of her television. The couch was warm and covered in chocolate brown velvet. They had purchased the couch together. It was their first joint purchase, and it was quite expensive. The woman put her head in his lap and cycled through the channels. She stopped for a few seconds to assess what was available on four and then took aim again, lurching them forward more rapidly through the remaining stations. After one go-round, she compromised, lowered her standards, and settled finally on a game show that asked regular people in regular American cities questions they should know the answers to but don't. Who said, Give me liberty or give me death? If someone's a zoologist, what do they study? What is TNT? That sort of thing. The host had all the answers and he egged the people on, encouraging them to elaborate on their misguided responses and typically bad hunches. Back in the studio, contestants placed their bets on who would get the questions wrong. Sometimes the contestants themselves answered incorrectly, doubling the fun. The audience, meanwhile, lapped up each incorrect response. The humiliation of one for the entertainment of many. There were a bunch of new shows just like this one.

The host was asking a blond couple in T-shirts and shorts—they wore identical outfits almost—who Napoleon was, and the man allowed, without too much reflection, that he was a sea captain, of course.

Good lord, the woman said.

The man on television wasn't positive, but he soon became more confident, spinning a whole seafaring life for the French emperor, while his wife, quieter than her voluble husband and happy to let him do all the talking, stood beside him, just nodding away. Napoleon, the man said, sailed around the world. His wife agreed without reservation.

Unbelievable, the boyfriend said. His girlfriend sat up and turned around so that her feet were in his lap now. Without a word he slipped her socks off and started kneading the balls of her feet with his hands. She cracked her toes on one foot and then the other.

The man on television was describing Napoleon's historic around-the-world voyage, when his wife, who had so far let her husband answer every question wrong, spoke for the first time. Wasn't Napoleon like Marco Polo? she asked. Her husband agreed immediately. Polo, he said, like Napoleon. The names fit together like lock and key. Na-polo-in. Napoleon, the man explained—for his wife was silent once more—was the famous blind sea captain who sailed around the world alone, in spite of his being blind.

This is incredible, the woman said.

Her boyfriend shrugged his shoulders as if to say how could she expect less than the absolutely incredible at two in the morning?

Where do they find these people? she asked. She wiggled the foot he wasn't working on, and he shifted his attention to it.

I like how certain this guy is, he said. He's plagued by zero doubt.

The man on television was expounding on the connection between the swimming-pool game children play and the rollicking ocean adventures of the great blind captain. His wife demonstrated, closing her eyes and saying, Marco, and her husband answered her, calling out, Polo. Marco, his wife said again. Just like that, the husband explained. The host then revealed that the couple was, in fact, wrong, and the audience, back in the studio, just laughed and laughed. Let's check the bidding, the host said, and with that the woman picked up the clicker and moved on.

That was amazing, her boyfriend said.

She put the clicker down and looked at him.

Watching that guy connect that stuff, watching him develop that connection between Napoleon and Marco Polo.

To be fair, she said, they weren't at all sure about it. They sounded pretty, you know, tentative.

Yeah, he said, but they became plenty sure of themselves. Did you see the look on that guy's face when his wife brought up Marco Polo?

She shook her head.

He was like, That's it! That's exactly right! The boyfriend tried to duplicate the look, to rearrange his face, but he was no actor. You would have thought they dug up a diamond in their backyard.

And then they both ran with it, she said.

Of course they ran with it, he said. It was their most promising lead.

They fell quiet, and she picked up the clicker again. When they came back around to the game show, the host was peppering the couple with questions about the French Revolution.

It's not fair to keep asking them these questions, she said. They obviously don't know their French history.

What's their specialty, you think? he said. Physics?

The channels blinked by quickly. There was a flash of blue, then a flash of green, then a flash of brown. The flashes of color sped up and then the flashes of color slowed down, until it seemed light itself was the new program.

That couple reminds me of Dorie and her fiancé, he said.

Oh, whatever, she said.

No, think about it, he said. They're both insulated from the world. They think they're right about Marco Polo, or they think it makes sense to eat steak and spinach every night and get engaged after, I'm sorry, one night of all-you-can-eat fried rice. To them, it all makes sense. It all makes perfect sense, you know?

The woman muted a black and white movie, some melodrama, and rolled onto her back, to face her boyfriend. She wasn't sure, she said, she saw things that way.

Come on, he said. You heard that story about the grandmother.

The woman shrugged. What about it?

I don't know, he said. It was kind of creepy, didn't you think? With the candles?

She was trying to entertain the kids, she said.

Candles are romantic, he told her.

She was just making them think the meal was something special, she said. And it worked.

Still appears to be working, he said.

The woman said whatever and went back to switching the channels.

You just know that guy is over there begging Dorie to dress up like his grandmother.

You're awful, the woman said. She swatted at her boyfriend with the remote. Just awful.

He was elaborating on a familiar idea of his, what he termed the Cocoon Theory of Human Relationships. The woman had heard it before. She had, in truth, heard it all before. The two of them had been together for years. Their families wondered what their plans were, as a couple, but had long ago lost interest in asking. Friends considered them married, in effect. In private, by themselves, they managed to avoid talking about marriage except as some vague project to finish up one day, someday. Their future was a herd of gazelles, which slipped by them, rushed ahead, and never glanced back.

Sometimes she wished they were married already. What was the big deal? And what were they waiting for? She didn't want a big to-do. Not anymore, anyway. A nice dress, something understated that she could wear again, a new pair of shoes, a couple of friends, and a courthouse would be just fine. She could even skip the shoes. I mean, really. She hadn't necessarily wanted to be engaged after a single date, like Dorie, a real slam-bang affair if ever there was one, but she now recognized its appeal, for sure. She saw the advantages. It was so certain. So unmistakable. It gripped her around the middle, a hand the height of her body squeezing her into a new shape. Just thinking about Dorie made her breathing go uneven, jagged.

According to the Cocoon Theory, as her boyfriend abbreviated it, every couple obeys a unique internal logic, in effect creating a little world of two, a world that can, potentially, bear little or no resemblance to the real world outside their cocoon. They don't doubt Napoleon was blind and also known by his nickname Marco Polo, because nobody is around them to suggest otherwise. They don't wonder too much about eating the same dinner every night, because being in the couple, as it were, being inside this warm, protective, climate-controlled cocoon, means that they almost never receive any countervailing information.

The boyfriend had many such theories. Another was that musical ability is inversely proportional to how much a musician moves his instrument when he plays. They weren't actually theories so much as a loose assortment of observations, personal preferences, and outright biases that he chose to dress up, dignifying with fancy names. Not that he ever hesitated to parade one of his theories out in minor triumph when some new observation confirmed the earlier scant evidence.

The woman asked her boyfriend, Are we in a cocoon?

He smiled and shrugged. Every couple has their own cocoon, he said. I'm not about to carve out some kind of special exemption for us. He rubbed the back of her little toe and then rubbed at the back of the next largest toe, and so on. The problem, he said, his voice getting slightly louder, as if a part of him believed he were addressing a conference room packed with appreciative scholars, or the danger, rather, is not the fact of the cocoon itself, but instead the thickness of the cocoon.

This is good, she said. He wasn't sure if she was speaking in earnest and meant the foot rub, or if she was teasing him, mocking his formulation of this new corollary, or clarification, to the Cocoon Theory.

Some cocoons are thin, he said, permitting ample light and information, or what have you, to reach the couple. He drew a breath and then moved her feet closer to him, to rub the tops. It unnerved him a bit when sincerity—simple sincerity—was not apparent, when

49

he couldn't even tell whether his girlfriend was kidding or serious as a stone. Was nothing ever truly clear between two people? It bore thinking about, but later. For now, he went on. And some cocoons, he said, are thick. He watched the flutter of his most cherished thoughts as they took wing. He liked how he spoke tonight. He even liked how his voice sounded. Some cocoons are so thick, air hardly gets through, and the couple— He looked gravely at his girlfriend. Over time, he said, that couple will die of chronic interpersonal asphyxiation.

It seems like a couple wouldn't know whether their cocoon was thick or thin, she said. I mean, how could they?

I don't know, he said. People should just have a sense for these things, I guess. People know.

What's your sense of our cocoon then? she said. Is our cocoon real thick, do you think?

Our cocoon, he said, is just right. There was, in his tone, a hint, however faint, of fairy tales, of stories told before bed to hasten sleep and dispel such questions and worries and concerns and ensure a good night's rest. He matched his thumb to her big toe and pressed the one against the other.

I'm being serious, she said.

I'm being serious, too, he said. We're fine. This cocoon, he said— he indicated their couch, the den, the apartment and walls around them—is just fine. She scared him. No, that wasn't it. He just never liked how their lightest conversations, at those moments when they were, both of them, at their most playful, could turn so dark, heavy, impossible. That's what scared him.

But how do you know? she said.

Because, he said, it's my theory. He had wanted to call the thing a stupid theory or, better, a stupid fucking theory, but he was still trying to keep things light. Was it too late for that? Probably so. His attempt hung in the air like a tiny, colorful cloud, suspended for just a second, until it sank under its own weight.

But you can't ever know, she said. That's the beauty of your theory.

He rubbed her feet harder, trying to work something out there or press something into her skin. He had always thought the theory's real beauty lay in the fun he derived from cracking wise about other people's problems under the guise of objective analysis and yes, from feeling slightly superior to them, better, or at least a little more aware. But he had some other point, too, though he couldn't just then get his mind around it. He couldn't quite figure out its shape. It was large, a mass of rock and twisted metal, the wreckage of an ancient collision he had happened upon by chance. It would be impossible for him alone to lift, so he sought some way—any way—to step back from the theory, putting some healthy distance, some useful distance, between him and it. It was never a real theory, anyway. It never had been. To call it a theory had been misguided, if not a bit grand, and she of all people knew well enough how he could, at times, be grand. He looked to his girlfriend and shrugged. He tried to smile, too, and he continued to rub. Why he rubbed—or when he might stop—he had no idea. His hands were tired. His fingers cramped, but he rubbed her feet as if the very action—the simple, repetitive, mindless motion—might lead him somewhere new.

You may be right, he told her.

PRAYER FOR WHAT WILL BE REVEALED

T HEY DISCOVERED the dead coyote in a cotton field behind their subdivision. The houses there were bordered on three sides by these fields and, on the fourth, by a fetid bayou with cattails and water as green as a pool table. He was supposed to be over playing with his friend, at his friend's house, when they found the animal. But his friend's house was on the edge of the subdivision, on the outside of the outermost street, so his backyard opened right into the fields. This was in the 1970s, in Louisiana, in a city built on the banks of the Red River.

The fields were nothing special, really, not to look at anyway. Just a lot of cotton. That suited them fine, though. It was someplace to go. They climbed the fence and then chased each other between the rows of plants. They played hide-and-seek and Marco Polo. The rows were so straight they sometimes ran with their eyes closed, holding their arms outstretched and letting their hands brush over the tops of the plants. They ran for what seemed to them like miles, and their shoes sank in the dirt with every step. The ground was soft, loamy, just this side of mud.

They decided that day to ride a bike through the field. The only bike the friend could get over the fence was his sister's, a small, pink number with long glittery tassels dangling from the ends of the handlebars. The friend got on first, but when he stood on the pedals, the bike just sank into the mud, so he hopped off and started running again.

Race you, the friend said.

For a second, he stayed behind and looked at the bike, motionless in the mud, like it was on display. Then he took off after his friend.

That was when they noticed the coyote. Its body was slit open from its neck to its tail, and its head was stuck on the end of a tall wooden pole driven into the ground. Thick waves of stink surrounded the body, and the friends were in the middle of the stench, right up by the carcass, before they knew quite what the thing was. From a distance it was merely something to run toward, some goal or destination. When they reached it, they would choose another. It had looked like a scarecrow. The farmer, whom nobody ever saw, had been known to put out scarecrows some years.

His friend bent over double and spit at the ground. He cupped his knees with his hands, then he dropped to all fours. I think I'm going to be sick, he said.

Cover your mouth, he told his friend. He pulled his T-shirt up over his neck and breathed through the material. The smell was still overpowering. When he was asked later what it smelled like, the only word that came to mind was memorable. It stuck in the mind like a thing with claws.

His friend crawled away, back toward his house, moaning and spitting as he went.

He stayed put, though, and studied the body. The smell didn't affect him. It was a putrid smell, to be sure, but it didn't make him retch. He stepped close to the carcass and circled around the pole. He could see now where the coyote had been cut open, how the flesh was ragged at the edges and the muscles hung off in thick ropes. The intestines lay in a pile, like a white hose, at his feet, and the organs glistened like jewels. He reached out to touch one—he didn't know what part. It was wet still.

His friend called out. What are you doing? He was standing fifty feet away by then.

Just looking, he said.

Come on, his friend said. Let's go.

What is it? he said.

What is it? his friend said. What do you mean? He couldn't believe the question. What is it? He started to walk back toward the body, but stopped. It's gross is what it is, he said. Now come on.

He looked up at the coyote's head. The pole raised it up a good six feet in the air, and the head hung down.

His friend said he was going, like now. It sounded like a last chance. His ultimatum stretched out to blanket their entire friendship, their past and future both.

He looked at the coyote's eyes then, really tried to look into them. There wasn't anything inside, not that he could see. They were all pupil and cloudy around the edges.

His friend kicked at a cotton plant and then spat once more at the ground. He was doing it for show now, to be dramatic. Come on, he said. Let's go already.

After a moment, he went. When they got back to his friend's house, they sat cross-legged in front of the TV and played Pong. They said not a word about what they'd seen. When they got bored, they went to his room. His friend picked up a pencil and drew a tic-tac-toe grid on the wall. He made an X in the center and then handed over the pencil.

The first time they had drawn on the walls—it must have been two years before, at least—he had asked, You sure this is okay?

His friend shrugged and said, We're renting.

That night, he went home and asked his mother and father what renting meant.

It means they don't give two shits, his father said.

They'll paint the walls is all it means, his mother said. Before they move.

He made an O in the lower right-hand corner, which for some reason was where he always played, and then handed the pencil back.

The game ended in cat, as it always did. They started a new game then, this time on a ten-by-ten grid, and played for a little while, until he said, I think I'll go home. His friend walked him to the door, and they said their see yous.

That night, as he lay in bed and tried to sleep, he saw the body of the coyote. Whether he shut his eyes or left them open, it didn't matter: the coyote looked down on him. Sometimes he could see himself standing before it, as if he were outside himself, standing to one side with a camera, recording their meeting for proof, or posterity. The thing he wondered was what it meant, the coyote. Or what it was for, first of all, and then what it meant. He was growing accustomed to the idea that everything had a meaning, sometimes two. Kids at school passed around these trading cards for the band Kiss, whose name everyone knew stood for Knights in Satan's Service. AC/DC meant Against Christ Devil's Children. And Adidas meant All Day I Dream about Sex. Kids repeated these secrets, passing them down to the younger generation like hard-won wisdom. The thing to do was just to act like he knew it all already, that he had heard it last summer or the grade before, whenever. Nobody knew what the coyote meant, he thought. Nobody could. Then he thought, Everyone will act as if it's no big deal, though. Dead coyote on a stick, right. He rolled over onto his back, laced his hands behind his head and stared at the ceiling. Records meant one thing one way, played normally, and then another when spun in reverse. So what, he wondered, would it mean to reverse the body of the coyote? It was a puzzle, and he decided maybe the solution lay beyond him.

He got out of bed then and went to the window. He walked with his hands outstretched, partly hunched over, picking his way in the dark like an old blind man. He tugged on the bottom of the shade and let in the light. The moon was high and passed into and out of a thin layer of clouds. He undid the lock on his window and opened it, at first a crack and then wider, wide enough so that he could rest his face on the sill and breathe in the air from outside. He didn't know what he was doing. If his mother or father walked in on him just then and asked, he could only answer that he didn't know. He really didn't know what he was doing.

The air was cool, cooler than he had supposed it would be, and didn't smell like anything he could put a name to, but he liked it just the same. It filled him up somehow, inflating him. He imagined drifting over the city, looking for someone else who was awake, looking for a small light on a bedside table, the blue glow of a TV set, a man in front of a toaster waiting for it to pop. He looked over at the house next door. All the windows were dark. Another friend of his once lived there, but then the family left town. It was abrupt. Nobody ever got the scoop on why they moved away. His mother told him he could write a letter to the old address, that the post office would forward it to his friend, and he did, he wrote a meandering letter about what was happening in school and what was on TV the night before and the night before that, and how he caught a lizard climbing on their old house, but he never got back any response.

Should try, he thought, to get some rest. He shut the window and went back to bed, leaving the shade up. He liked the moonlight, he decided. The color of it, how it made everything look cold.

It was like camping under the stars, sort of. When he was finally too tired to do anything other than sleep, he dreamed of coyotes, outside, pacing around. There were dozens of them, maybe more. The world was full of coyotes. They were quiet animals, stealthy, but he could hear them still. They rubbed their fur against the house as they brushed past in the night.

PRAYER FOR THE FIRST BALANCE

SOMETHING HAPPENED when they got back from the grocery store. She dropped the bags where she stood, and he continued on into the kitchen. He made it a point not to look back. He told himself, Right now, I'm not looking back at her. My back is to her, and I'm not going to look back.

She said she wanted to talk about what they each did. She wanted to talk about investment. This was not about money, though that was part of it. If he asked, Is this about money? she'd say it's not just about money. She'd say, Don't be so reductive. I'm talking about your emotional investment, too.

He started to put the groceries away. They were in his apartment, where everything had its place. Grandma's house, she called it. He put the chips away on a middle shelf, the rice away in another place. Then he became inspired to rearrange the freezer.

It was as he was putting the soup away, in the last cupboard on the highest shelf, that he knocked a plant over, one of two jades he was growing. It fell off the sill, and the pot cracked into a half dozen pieces. He had just watered his plants that day, so the soil was pretty wet. When the plant hit the ground, wet dirt went every which way, splattering. The plant did not fall because they were fighting. She did not make him bump into the pot. He was not so frazzled that he couldn't stack the cans of soup. It did not happen because they were fighting; however, it did happen while they were fighting, and that's the way he'll remember it.

Later, he will think that the plant, when it hit the ground, didn't make much noise: there was only a light thud and then pieces sprayed across the floor. Ideally, it should have made more noise, he thought. Or something.

He did not clean up the mess, not right away. Instead, they sat in the other room and talked. It was hard for him to ignore that on the other side of the wall there was a mess that needed to be cleaned up, put into order. Yes, his mind focused on what she was saying and what he was trying to say, but part of it was also back in the kitchen, already collecting pieces of the pot, sweeping up the dirt, and balancing the remainder of the plant back on the sill.

It was at least two hours before she went home to her apartment and he got back into the kitchen. The wet dirt had dried by then. He would need to scrub. While he ran the water in the tub, waiting for it to get hot enough, he stood at the threshold of the kitchen and surveyed the mess.

There's a story artists tell about accidents. In Philadelphia, in the art museum, there's a work made of two large pieces of glass, with some wire, paper, and more fragile materials sandwiched between them. When a team of movers was carrying the work out of the artist's studio, to transport it to the museum, one of the sheets of glass broke. Nobody knew how it happened. The movers were professionals, and the work was well padded, packed into a custom-made crate and treated with tenderness and care. And yet when they unpacked the work at the museum, they found it broken. A web of deep cracks began at the center and shot out toward all four sides of the frame. Spotlights illuminated the work from above, and the crack just glowed. Upon seeing the damage, the artist, who was there to help with the installation, pronounced that his work was now complete.

In the bathroom, he filled a pail with soap and hot water. He never believed this story about the artist. It seemed, at some level, an unlikely reaction. And yet, when he looked at his plant on the ground, arms of spattered soil reaching for his stove, his refrigerator, the table, and his door, he did feel the temptation, however slight, to make a similar pronouncement: now this is complete. He realized, though, that to say so is to express many things, not one of them satisfaction that now everything is right and all is done. Perhaps the artist was too tired to make things how they once were. Isn't that more likely? It was like that time she told him, I can't do this anymore. I'm too tired to care.

He knelt down in the kitchen and scrubbed at the floor with a brush. The floor didn't look this way before, but he had in his mind a picture of how it was. He was haunted by his memory of the first balance, that time when things were just so. Doing something over is the real work of this life. Two times, three times, it doesn't matter how many: doing something over is our real work.

PARABLE OF THE THREAD

I WAS TOLD TO give up looking for my grandmother. I was told she was lost. Gone for good. After two-and-a-half weeks of trying to follow the red thread looped three times around her waist, I heard from friends, neighbors, and officials all separately positing that her red thread was now irretrievably tangled with the other threads out there, ones looped three times and tied around other grandmothers and grandfathers, themselves also gone for good. I was told these things also by my family, who wanted me at home, they said, to lead the nightly grace and attend to some other unspecified tasks: gutter-cleaning, more than likely, or wallpaper removal, or maybe moving heavy objects from high shelves. My wife heard it said that to search for so long was simply not advisable. They presented her with cautionary tales and knowing glances.

I pray for faith, in both my grandmother, who could be irascible in her own way, and the red thread, which seemed sturdy enough. I looped it around her one night while she slept. Lacking a real icon or even a photograph of her, I direct my prayers toward her favorite chair. A stocky reading table sits beside it, piled with cooking magazines, community newsletters, and a crossword puzzle dictionary. On the other side is a great spool of red thread. It unwinds through the living room, out the entry hall, and under the door. The spool buzzes slightly, barely, as it turns. It has not stopped unwinding since she left. In some circles, this is interpreted, however cautiously, as a good sign.

I am not alone in my searching. There are many of us out here tracking threads, hunting grandmamas and grandpapas. We are professionals, some of us, and first-timers, others; we have one thing on our minds: find our elderly, find them before we are elderly, too, and tied fast with thread. We search out of love, yes, of a sort, but also fear, fear of being gone for good like they are gone for good.

Would you believe I met a woman out here? She was also following a line of red thread, if you can believe that. Down the same street as me even. Coincidence was our first attraction. When the excitement of coincidence flagged, we discovered something else to take its place: We both love coffee!

Now we are sitting at a sidewalk cafe. It is little! It is delightful! It is the sort of place made expressly for the words little and delightful. We've been here for days, though we swear to each other it has seemed like weeks, for we know each other so well. We are ordering all the desserts, one at a time, from the little menu. The waiter promises every item is delightful. He loves them all, he says. We ask him for two forks, and he brings us two plates. No, forks, we say, and then we laugh. We want to share, you see?

We are leaning over our table and speaking so that only we can hear. Underneath, our knees rub. We each hold one hand out and let the threads slip through our fingers. If you didn't know better, you'd think we were merely relaxing, that's how casual we appear. This searching cannot be rushed. Though we occasionally touch each other (on the arm, on the face) and even have a bit of a kissy thing going, we never let loose the threads. We are careful that way, cautious even. We tell each other we want love, and we mean it, we think, in a way.

The threads run on, unwinding, and the desserts just keep coming. My God, this torte! It's great. This carrot cake and the crème brûlée. Waiter! Oh, waiter!

PRAYER FOR THOSE WHO LONG

HER FIRST STEREO had a receiver, an eight-track tape player, and a turntable. The receiver and turntable were housed in simulated wood-grain cabinetry. The manufacturer had put stickers to that effect on both components: For appearance and overall durability this stereo is housed in simulated wood grain. She and her brother played that stereo loud. When they got a pair of microphones, they pretended to be musicians and recorded themselves playing their guitars. They made up songs. For lyrics, they read copy from clothing catalogs. There was the pants song, the hiking boots song, and songs she didn't remember anymore. Sometimes they just made noise. Once, she recorded the sounds of her brother attempting to tune in a distant radio station. Whatever they recorded, they played it back really loud. They cranked it up. That was the parlance of the day, anyway. One local radio station had these DJs who were forever urging listeners to crank it up. Sometimes they opened all the windows and moved the speakers so that the sounds carried down the street. Whenever people walked by, she and her brother observed them, watching to see how they reacted. Had they liked their latest recording? Did they enjoy the singing? Did they appreciate the playing? It was, in the end, hard to say for sure, as the passersby pretended not to hear.

PARABLE OF ANOTHER'S SHOES

Beckett even wore pointed-toe patent leather pumps that were too small because he wanted to wear the same shoe in the same size as Joyce, who was very proud of his small, neatly shod feet. Joyce had been vain about his feet since his youth, when poverty forced him to go about Dublin in a pair of white tennis shoes, the only footwear he owned.

DEIRDRE BAIR
Samuel Beckett: A Biography

DOWN ON STAGE there is a play going on. My neighbor, whom I don't know from Adam, leans way over toward me and speaks into my ear. Hey, he says, why don't you put yourself in my shoes?

I look down at the floor. His shoes are unlaced. His feet are resting on top of them. He's flexing his toes in his socks. One with a hole.

I look back at the stage. This play's been going on for some time. I think, Sure, why not. So I move to drag his shoes toward me.

Wait, he says. Put yourself in my seat before you put yourself in my shoes.

You want to trade seats, too? I ask.

My neighbor nods and then he's talking to the person to his immediate right. Finally he looks back at me.

Who's that lady beside you? he asks.

I look to my left. I turn back to my neighbor. I don't know, I say.

My neighbor says, You got to talk to her.

Why? I ask.

He looks at me blankly. We're all moving to the right. She's going to have to put herself in your shoes. Go, he says. Make arrangements.

And so I do.

By the fourth act I'm sliding around in my neighbor's wingtips. My neighbor is wedged into a pair of sequined pumps. His skin, his sock, the fat of his foot, droop over the top of the pump like a muffin. Everywhere I look: incongruity. The woman in the off-the-shoulder gown, in cowboy boots; the man in the tweed jacket, in espadrilles; the boy in his father's shoes; the husband in his wife's; his wife now in two-tone tasseled loafers.

After the play there's a dance for all of us and our new shoes. I find the woman who relinquished her zip-up half-boots for my black dress shoes (bought for a funeral, distant relative) and I ask her to dance. I take her by the hand to right out in front of the band. This is not a learning experience, I can't ignore that. We all *want* to like each other's shoes and we all *want* to fit in and play along and go with the flow, but none of us can ignore the discomfort. I started out thinking, What a great idea! How simply whimsical! When the play ended, however, and I still didn't have my shoes back, I thought, Who will believe me when I tell them? Now, the dancing has reached its tenth hour. There are rumors circulating that we'll be trading again before the night's out, to try yet one more person's shoes. It's hard not to be disgusted.

I am uncomfortable. I can't keep my mind off that.

Where does this discomfort go? Up toward the ceiling, with the music? Into our drinks? When we excuse ourselves to the restroom are we hoping to lose it in the plumbing or rinse it from our mouths? Me, I solemnly dance this discomfort away, or try at least. I am not alone in my endeavor: many of us take to the floor. We ignore the person who has our shoes or whose shoes we wear and dance, dance, dance. We dance in the modern style, we look down at the floor, at our feet, and watch ourselves move.

PRAYER FOR THE FATHER

M<small>Y MOTHER</small> met me at the door. Your father baked another loaf of bread today, she said. Just so you know.

I nodded and went to the kitchen to get a snack. Chips and onion dip. The new loaf of bread was on the counter, cooling atop a wire rack. It was impressive, and larger than most of what he baked. A pair of those, I thought, would make a nice set of speakers.

So how did school go? my mother said.

I shrugged. All right, I guess.

My brother was in the den, stretched out on the couch watching television. Dad made more bread, he said. He rubbed his stomach in a tiny circle. Do you want three slices? he asked. Or should I get you four?

He baked another loaf of bread today. He baked another loaf of bread.

At dinner, our father put the day's bread on the table and then offered to cut us a slice. He followed many different recipes. He made many different kinds.

Our father was marking the time, occupying himself. For six months and then six more, he had been out of work, looking for work. My brother and I helped him however we could. We typed his résumé. We composed his cover letters.

In school, in American government class, kids argued the merits of welfare. One guy, a sort of friend, said all these deadbeats just need to get jobs already. At the front of the classroom, the teacher had hung a portrait of George Washington. Next to it was a headshot of John Wayne.

Today our father baked another loaf of bread.

We had many loaves then.

PRAYER FOR SOMETHING SEEN
BUT BRIEFLY

THE CARETAKER at the campground told the father and his daughter that he had recently found a strange animal in the woods. He wasn't sure what it was, but he was willing to show them, he said, if they were interested. The father looked at his daughter and asked what she thought. She shrugged and nodded. She would check it out, sure. Why not? she said.

The caretaker motioned for them to follow him into the back. I keep it in my office, he said.

His office was more of a bedroom that happened to have a desk. The room was small and dimly lit and needed a good airing out. Though it was late in the afternoon, the shades were pulled. What sunlight shone in made everything look brown, like an old family photograph. The caretaker rooted around beneath his desk, removed a box, and placed it on top. The box measured three feet on each side and opened in such a way that the father and daughter couldn't see in. The caretaker removed a cloth bag of some sort— dark green, made of velvet perhaps—and placed it on the ground. Then he closed the box and moved it out of the way.

You ready? he asked.

The daughter shrugged and nodded. It was almost all she ever did. She was the world-weariest of eight-year-olds.

With that, the caretaker hefted the bag up to his waist and balanced it against his thigh. Then he untied a rope from the mouth of the bag. Take a look, he said.

The daughter leaned over the desk. The father leaned over the daughter's shoulder. The daughter thought she saw something in the bag, some long claw maybe, perhaps some fur and a flash of white. It looked like no animal she'd ever seen, but then she couldn't see it well, whatever it was. She felt her father's breath on the back of her neck and wanted to leave. Her father said, What's the big idea here? He looked at the caretaker as if he knew what he'd been shown and was not pleased. In reality, he didn't know. He was just the suspicious type.

The caretaker said, No big idea, just something I found. Like I told you.

The daughter asked if they could camp now, and her father said, Sure, of course, let's go.

The caretaker followed them outside and told them to enjoy their stay. Seems like you brought good weather with you, he said.

Later, after they had unpacked the car and set up their pup tents, the daughter asked her father what the deal had been with that caretaker anyway.

Him? the father said. Just some weird old man, playing a stupid joke, I guess.

But what was that thing? the daughter asked.

The father said he wasn't sure. He hadn't gotten a good look either. The guy had barely opened the bag, he said. And it was so dark in there. Nevertheless, the father had managed over the last few hours to pretty well convince himself that it was the old man's penis they had seen. It sounded crazy, the father knew it did, but that was the only way he could add it all up. The guy was some weird old pervert. The world was full of them.

The father had a mind to do something, of course, or say something, but he hadn't wanted to make a scene in front of his daughter and ruin the whole weekend. He got to see her so seldom as it was.

When it was time for bed, he tucked his daughter into her

sleeping bag and kissed her on the forehead. Good night, he said. We'll have more fun tomorrow. He had been telling her that since she was small, since before she could talk. He didn't know why he said it, or even how he came up with it. It sounded like something a cartoon rabbit on a children's program would say before signing off. Remember, kids, we'll have more fun tomorrow. It was a powerful habit, though, and he could see no reason to break it.

The father went to his tent and sat awake, considering his options. After more than an hour of stewing, he crept outside and then walked up the road toward the caretaker's house. The forest was dark and still. Every noise he made sounded loud, an imposition on the quiet.

No lights were on at the caretaker's, but the father knew he was home. He had to be. Where else would a guy like that go in a place like this? A gravel driveway led to the house, and the father skirted its edge, wanting to avoid alerting the old man to his presence. When he reached the house, he sank low to the ground and snuck around back, to where the office/bedroom was. The father had no plan, just this feeling he needed to do something. It was like an outline of an idea he would fill in as he went along. The father knocked on the window several times. Then he stopped and listened. When he didn't hear anything, he knocked again, louder this time. Then, with the flat of his hand, he hit the window frame, rattling all the panes. He stopped once more and listened. The father thought he heard something faint, a stirring, but he wasn't sure.

I know you're in there, he said. He spoke conversationally, as if the old man were just sitting on the other side of the shade, as he may well have been. You want to step outside? the father said. I need to have a word with you. Now.

He heard no noises within, nothing.

Fucking coward, he said. Fucking pervert coward.

The father went around to the front door and tried the knob. It was locked. He wasn't sure what he would have done if he had found it unlocked. He imagined himself, though, pushing the door open, all the way, and leaving it like that, his calling card: I could have come right inside and done what, I do not know. How the father would have loved to have seen the old man's face when he woke up and found his door wide open. How puzzled he would be.

The father pounded and kicked at the door. Open this door, he said. After a few minutes, when the old man didn't emerge, the father gave up and started to walk away, back to camp. Of course, that's when the old man decided finally to show himself. He came around from behind the house and climbed up onto his porch. You got something you need to say to me, son? he said.

The old man was wearing what clothes he wore when they were checking in. The father supposed he must sleep that way. Like a drunk does, he thought. He walked back to where the old man stood. As he was about to set foot on the porch, the old man said that was far enough.

Fuck off, the father said, and he stepped onto the porch.

Such language, the old man said. You talk like that around your little girl?

Skip the lecture, reverend. You know why I'm here.

The old man said he hadn't the foggiest.

Well, I think you do, the father said. Because I didn't appreciate that little display you put on for my daughter this afternoon.

Was she scared by it? the old man said.

No, I wouldn't say that, the father said.

Well, then, the old man said, no harm, no foul, sounds like.

You exposed yourself, the father said. To my daughter.

Cool your jets, son, the old man said. I did no such thing.

I know what I saw, the father said.

The old man laughed. Okay, he said, man knows what he saw. Now, how about you get off my porch and go?

The father looked at him and shifted his weight from one leg to the other. He was tired, tired of being out here, talking. He hadn't come to debate.

Get some sleep, the old man said. It'll straighten out your mind.

That right? the father said.

The old man shrugged elaborately, as if he were slipping free of chains. That's my experience, yes.

What you did was wrong, the father said. I don't care what you tell yourself, it was wrong.

The old man waved the father off. He had heard enough. Get out of here, he said. He said it like he was frightening away a mangy cat.

The father stepped off the porch. He would go all right, but not because he was told. There just was no point in continuing. Still, he hated turning his back on the old man. He would have liked to have walked backwards until he could no longer see him. Instead, he felt like he was surrendering or, worse, agreeing to disagree.

He reached the end of the driveway, and the old man called out to him. What kind of father leaves his daughter in the middle of the woods?

When he returned to their camp, the daughter was inside his tent, crying. She had woken up, she said. She heard something, some sound, she wasn't sure what. She called to him, over and over, and when he didn't answer, she figured he was sleeping, and so she unzipped her tent and went to his, but he was gone. She had wanted to sleep in his tent, just for tonight, but he was gone.

The father held his daughter to his body and said he was sorry. He held her head to his shoulder and he kissed her crown. Her hair, the smell, reminded him of giving her baths when she was a baby. How clean she would emerge, and how the bathroom smelled like her, even after she was asleep. He found the smell around the house, too. It was always a surprise to him, how the smell attached itself to his clothes, to a towel, even to their blanket, where she lay for just a few minutes. He breathed her smell in and let it fill him up. My baby, he thought.

Where were you? she said.

He hated to lie to her, of course. He had promised himself—told himself—to raise her on the truth, no excuses and no exceptions, no matter what, but then he broke that promise and then he just kept breaking it. I went for a walk, he said.

At night?

I couldn't sleep, he said. I don't know why.

The daughter nodded and then climbed into his sleeping bag. She squirmed for a bit, but then she settled down. I don't like it here, she said.

Well, let's give it a chance, okay?

All right, she said. The daughter had a way of making all right sound like whatever.

We could take a walk tomorrow, the father said. He was trying. He wanted to find in the dull rock of the weekend a thin vein of gold. Even a few flecks would do.

You mean at night? she said. She sounded horrified, but it may have been mock horror, playing it up. He wasn't sure. More and more, he couldn't tell with her.

If you want, he said. Sure.

It's so dark, she said. Outside.

Your eyes will adjust, he said.

PRAYER FOR THE APPEARANCE OF
SOMETHING GERMAN

ONE SUMMER, she taught her boyfriend German. She was not German herself and hadn't taken a class in some years. Nor had she traveled to Germany or had one occasion to speak the language, but still she knew the basics cold. He asked her how that could be, and she said she dreamed in German. People in her dreams spoke to her in German, and she answered them, also in German.

The boyfriend started carrying a notebook to write down the phrases she taught him. He learned the alphabet and the numbers. He learned hello and good-bye. He learned to say, How are you? as well as a variety of possible responses. When they went to the ice-cream place, she taught him phrases relevant to the experience of the ice-cream place. How much is a vanilla cone, please? I would like two scoops. No chocolate syrup for me, thank you. When they went downtown, they pretended to be lost German tourists.

Months later, a clerk in a department store approached them. I'm sorry to bother you, she said. But are you from Germany?

They were surprised. The question was just, as they say, so random. She hadn't been teaching him any new words, and he hadn't been practicing any of the handful of phrases he'd committed to memory.

Yes, she told the clerk, we are German, in fact. How funny you should ask.

The boyfriend nodded and turned to a rack of clothes, trying just to look occupied.

The clerk looked at them both and smiled, pleased. I thought so, she said. You had that whole different look about you.

PARABLE OF BEING INSIDE

T HE NEW NIGHTCLUB opened last week, and now everyone is
trying to get inside. The new nightclub is fabulous, according
to every indication, offering entertainment beyond measure, joy
and conviviality in unparalleled quantities. Consider the new night-
club's stereo. Its sound system, speakers, mixing board, and turn-
tables are together larger, more expensive, and more powerful than
the stereos of the top five most popular nightclubs combined. The
stereo's wiring would, if stretched end to end, run for seventy-seven
miles, connecting cities to their suburbs. It loops underground,
beneath the glass dance floor, and then circles overhead, in the raf-
ters and around the exposed beams of the building, which, once
upon a time, was a warehouse or a tannery, a potato chip company
or dress shoe factory, something, in any case, that did something
for someone, back when. Nobody can remember now. The new
nightclub's wire is bound together in thick, menacing coils, blue
wires and black wires all feeding into intricately webbed nodes and
impressive muscular bunches. It is as if the club powered itself off
the flayed body of a giant. The new nightclub's blue wire is the blue
of four a.m. seen before sleep; its black wire is truly black indeed.

I haven't yet been inside the new nightclub when it's turned on,
when the lights are up and people pack the open spaces and drinks
are being drunk. During the day, I worked on the second auxil-
iary electrical crew, brought onboard by one of the subcontractors,
this guy I know who used to date my sister. I wired up a set of
lights mounted on these robotic arms, metal appendages, starved

in appearance, that supported these other things that someone else, hired by another subcontractor, worked on.

The DJ booth in the new nightclub can unleash various special effects, the sort that would not seem out of place in large-budget movies. I've heard talk of lasers and holograms, even green screens. Supposedly parts of the club can be rear-projected into whole other areas, like scenery. Also, the bar is actually three bars, three bars each on three separate levels, each decorated according to unique styles or moods. The owner of the new nightclub is a stickler for details, so the moods of the bars are very much like the moods of people, very lifelike.

The new nightclub is where the old nightclub used to be, before it closed its doors, boarded the windows, and sold off all the furniture and stereo equipment in an auction sparsely attended by bargain hunters and just some curious lookers-on who felt they had some connection to the place. Nothing from the old nightclub survives in the new one.

People who have never even given a thought to going to a nightclub feel the inkling or perhaps pressure of having to go to this one, of needing to go, if only to see it, maybe just once. To see what it's like, they say. For something to do, they say. They all have their reasons, and their reasons are the same three or four.

It's a childish wish, this desire to be inside the new nightclub. Childish not in the sense of being simple, but rather because it reminds me of times I overheard my parents and their friends at parties. It was usually someone's birthday or anniversary, the occasion was never all that clear or important. What mattered was that I could hear their voices, the sound of their voices, but I could not discern the words themselves. I would hear laughter and I would think, Someone just told a joke. Who told a joke? Who was it? What was the joke, exactly? How did it go? The laughter went on. Laughter carried, words did not. I could hear nothing except sounds of what I knew to be conversation. It was incredibly frustrating, this feeling.

Inside the new nightclub there is another, smaller, more exclusive nightclub, and inside that smaller, more exclusive nightclub, there is a smaller nightclub still. Five nightclubs at least are nested inside one another like so. After work one day, a few days before we finished and the foreman, as they say, let us go, I was talking to a guy who worked alongside me, this guy who put the things on the ends of the metal appendages I was working on. Anyway, this guy swore that there are at least nine nested nightclubs inside one another. He personally knew of at least nine, and he suspected there could be even more, each smaller, each more exclusive, each located inside the other. And at the center of it all, at the center of this series of clubs within clubs, there is a room, supposedly no bigger than a large box, like the sort of box a refrigerator comes packaged in. The owner of the new nightclub has had this room decorated sparsely, with a table and a chair and a candle on the table and a pillow on the chair. The table is not larger than a pad of paper. The candle is the size of a dime. The chair is plain. The pillow is more suggestion and gesture than pillow. What's more, the walls around the table are not in fact walls. On closer inspection, they reveal themselves to be speakers that look and feel like walls. Solid speakers. From the floor to the ceiling of the room, nothing but speakers. When the stereo is on, and the music is going, a person admitted to the room that lies at the center of the series of clubs within clubs can hear nothing else, nothing to indicate that there's anything else anywhere else outside or inside the room, nothing other than the room itself and the person inside it.

PRAYER BY CLAUDIUS, KING OF DENMARK, WHO RECONSIDERS HIS EARLIER ATTEMPT AT PRAYER AND, WITH THE BENEFIT OF HINDSIGHT BESTOWED ON HIM BY THE AFTERLIFE, ENTERTAINS AND CRAFTS CERTAIN RHETORICAL IMPROVEMENTS

MY AFTERLIFE is carpeted, but not lavishly so. The carpet covers a hallway without end or start. The walls of this hallway meet the ceiling not in sharp, defined corners, but in a gentle, consistent curve. The same is true of the floor, where the carpet can be said to wash up the wall approximately three to four hands on either side, as though the carpet were a grayish blue wave that never recedes or crests.

The hallway is wide and tall enough to permit, just barely, a carriage and a team of horses to pass. On second thought, the carpet may be more accurately described as bluish gray. At any rate, the walls are unadorned. My colleagues tell me the lighting is fluorescent. I have reason to believe there once were windows along this hallway, or openings of some sort, but now there is only and everywhere wall, with some patches that look like newer construction. The hallway is not without these and other minor flaws in workmanship, but overall it's quite solid. On third thought, I now think the carpet is transparent, wholly free of color. It feels like carpet, but possesses no hue.

I do not know for certain whether this hallway represents hell or heaven. I have good reason to suspect the former, given what details of my life I can still recall, but the fact that I can't be said to know, really, one way or another and, furthermore, that nobody else around here knows either, one way or another, gives me some little hope. Might the hallway lead somewhere? I wonder. And might that place, this hypothetical location where the hallway terminates, relieve me eventually of my uncertainty? Perhaps. But so where, then, does this hallway go to? To what ultimate destination? A well-appointed great room? Somewhere with a vaulted ceiling, possibly? And maybe candles, tall as men, positioned on a thick slab of a table? O what I would not give for a table groaning under the weight of a feast! O what I would not pledge for such food! A meal! Even a simple one, bereft of garnish, produced without flourish, and prepared with neither skill nor care!

But I have walked this hallway for quite some time now and not yet seen any indication that it terminates anywhere, in a room great or otherwise. There was a time, this was long ago, that I resolved to walk only to my left. I walked as far as I could, and when I neared the point when my collapse seemed all but imminent, I sat down and I rested, and when I needed to sleep, I made sure to fall asleep with one arm outstretched and my body pointed headfirst in the direction I would resume walking once I awoke.

I never saw a single thing. Not one. I tired finally of walking only to my left and began at once walking only to my right. Eventually, I didn't care which way I walked. Right, left, it mattered not at all. Some days I spent pacing from wall to wall. Some days I chose not to walk.

I have not seen the prince. I had thought I would, at some point, see him. I thought the prince would be around, as it were, if not with me, then walking the hallway alone, or perhaps coming in the opposite direction down the same hallway. I can almost picture him, walking. As he passes, I reach out and grab him around the wrist. I say hello. When he turns toward me, I see it is, in fact, the prince, just as I remember him. He looks at me funny, though, and says I must be mistaken.

The truth is, I have no need for a feast or even, for that matter, a simple meal. I've been relieved by death of the need to eat, and yet I still dream of eating well. The need to eat in order to breathe and live has vanished, and yet the fantasy of dining pleasantly still persists and retains some residual charge. Curious how that works.

I'm starting to suspect this hallway may, in fact, represent hell. I just am not sure it represents heaven is the thing. At some point, the process of elimination has to take over. Or so one supposes. Unless the belief that heaven will be so heavenly and hell so very hellish is, in fact, so much wishful thinking, which is something else I've started to suspect. Because it's a useful myth, is it not? This notion that a person will know, instantly, upon arrival, I am in heaven. Or what have you. In general, I've found, there is so much wishful thinking, so much to be disabused. It's hard to know where to begin, frankly.

Consider the highly contrastive afterlife, with its sharp distinctions between hell and heaven. Such a model exists to warn the living, perhaps even to scare them, the children especially. It encourages them to reform their ways, improve their conduct, choose the right path and so forth. For those not presently living, however, for us, the dead, such distinctions are but wasted efforts, like ornate scenery constructed for a drama one has no choice except to sit through, enduring it, forever.

I could be wrong, of course, but I've spent not a few hours worrying some holes in this problem.

I have ample time to pray, though I honestly do not know why I bother. I once believed prayer had but two distinct functions, both in their essence requests. First, there are those who might pray in order to request that they be saved before they fall, sin, deceive, lie, cheat, murder, what have you. Then there are those who might pray in order to request that they be pardoned after they have fallen, stolen, murdered, misrepresented, dissembled, et cetera, et cetera. Those two functions are not by any means incorrect, but to them I have now added a third. There are those who might pray simply because others around them pray. I can report that my colleagues here pray a great deal, and I do join them from time to time, often for no better reason than to join someone somewhere at something halfway tangible. The point is I bow my stubborn knees and simulate prayer. Our words, whether mumbled and muttered or called out or cried, fly up as they ever did. Our thoughts, however complex they may be, however veined with our biases, remain below. As ever.

Could I have prayed harder? I could. And could I have stayed with it for some unspecified longer period of time? Greater duration could have done me little harm. And could I have concentrated? Until my forehead, when I had a forehead, wrinkled as my brain, when I possessed a brain, was wrinkled. And could I have phrased my words more particularly or, better to say, more precisely, so that their sound and force reached whomever it is who listens to such sounds from the likes of those such as me? Certainly. And if I had, if I had done all that and perhaps implemented six or seven or eight or nine other alterations besides, would I be here, in this place? Would I be lying facedown on this carpet for God knows how long? I don't know. That I do not know.

I am, incidentally, very near to announcing the discovery of a fourth function of prayer. I now believe that prayer may be the noise a person otherwise unoccupied makes. Prayer is the sound of a being doing very little being at all.

Gertrude is around here, somewhere, I believe. I think I see her from time to time. I wave to her, but she pretends not to see me. Perhaps she isn't pretending. It's entirely possible that she may not be able to see. Sometimes Gertrude is praying, sometimes walking the hallway like the rest of us. It's been a bit since I saw Gertrude last. How much time is impossible to say. I have no sense.

The horses are approaching! The noise of their nearing fills the hallway just as their smell announces their recent departure. It can only be the horses, pulling their carriage, driven by the driver and staffed by his hirelings. They pass by with some regularity. How often, exactly, is, like much else, impossible to say.

My colleagues and I must huddle up against the walls to allow the carriage sufficient room. Even then I feel the horses brush against me, smell the driver's breath (beer, garlic), and see his men leering at me, leering at us, with expressions that mix equal quantities of taunt and hate and curiosity. Men and women who do not move out of the way quickly enough are crushed under the hooves and wheels and are, over time, ground into the carpet.

On occasion, the driver calls for the horses to stop. Hold up, he says. Hold up, he says again. The horses shift in their gear, shuffle their hooves, and relieve themselves on the carpet. The carriage creaks. Then the driver points to some man or gestures in the direction of some woman, some unfortunate walking this hallway with me, and says, Do you know whose birthday it is today? He's asking the hirelings. The question is strictly rhetorical, but the men all shake their heads in a hammy fashion. No, we sure don't know whose birthday it is. They know well enough. They all know. The driver pauses for effect and then points again to the man or gestures once more to the woman. And with that, the whole staff and he begin singing, Happy birthday to you. Happy birthday to you. . . .

My colleagues and I debate the nature of their singing. They intend the song insincerely, that much is clear. It is meant, if it is meant at all, as a mockery of intimacy and friendship. But does their singing bear any correlation to our actual birthdays? Does the singing, though sarcastic, nonetheless mark the passage of another year? Is the driver even accurate about whom he points out? Or do they sing their song, aiming it in a random manner, at any one of us? Some birthdays come frequently; some seem not to come at all.

As the song ends, the driver applies his whip to his horses with undisguised ferocity, and they're off again, down the hall, to sing at someone else all over again. I have read that the most inexcusable and disgraceful of all noises is the cracking of whips—a truly infernal thing when it is done in the narrow resounding streets of a town. Arthur Schopenhauer. On Noise. He was after my time. Make no mistake, the sound is no better in a carpeted hallway without end or beginning. I have read, from the same source, No one with anything like an idea in his head can avoid a feeling of actual pain at this sudden, sharp crack, which paralyzes the brain, rends the thread of reflection, and murders thought. But then, all murderers murder thought, in a way, in a sense, if one were to think about it, which I do, from time to time.

PRAYER FOR THE SECOND OPINION

ONLY LATER did my father mention the doctors. We were chatting on the phone, talking about the weekend, about what he had done and what he was working on. I call every week almost—or I try at least—usually on Sundays. He told me he drove the riding mower around the yard, picking up and mulching all the fallen leaves. I have to do this at least once each week, my father said. Or else the leaves pile up and kill the grass underneath. He described how, after he had finished and stored the mower back in the shed, he took a large pine cone and spread peanut butter and seeds over all its scales and hung it from a tree limb. Something for the birds this winter, he said. He described this in great detail, elaborating on his every step. He spoke specifically, with a certain authority and a command over both what he did and what he was now saying. As he spoke, he yawned a couple of times. I had called later than usual.

My father told me then how he softened the peanut butter in the microwave, just heating it a little bit at a time and checking it, so that it finally softened enough to pour like a syrup, yet was not so hot as to separate the oil from the peanut butter. He spread the peanut butter over the pine cone then. This is one of those large pine cones, my father explained. I'm sure you remember them. I'm sure you can picture them. They stand probably eight or nine inches tall, at least. They weigh a couple of pounds, nearly. These are California pine cones. I brought a few of them back with me when I visited California. I never knew what to do with them.

After coating the scales and crevices of the pine cone with peanut butter, my father spooned birdseed onto it. Then he held the pine cone in his hands and rolled it around in the birdseed that had fallen off. Most of the birdseed stuck. The peanut butter was still warm and gummy and soft. The birds will love this, my father said. I'm sure they'll love it. Your mother already saw a goldfinch standing on top of the pine cone. If the finches don't start to eat it, he said, I'll take it down from the tree and put it on the ground, where the squirrels can have at it. I'll give the birds a couple of weeks, then it's the squirrels' turn. Someone is going to love it.

My father yawned again. I said, So what's the plan for this week? I was curious to hear about what he would do at work come Monday.

The company he worked at was building eight hundred towers to support windmills, and I enjoyed hearing about that project. I wanted to hear how the windmills were coming, how many they had already made, how many they had shipped, and where they would be constructed once completed. I pictured dozens of these towers together, planted on a hillside, in long rows. Dozens of windmills made a wind farm, when they were all together. One day, I imagined, I'll go to see a wind farm. Or maybe I'll just happen to travel past one while heading somewhere else. Whatever the case, I'll have to pull off the road and look at the windmills spinning atop the hill. At first, I might not know why I'm stopping. But then I'll remember as best as I can what my father told me about the towers.

My father knew the weights of the individual pieces that comprised the towers, the time it took to manufacture them, the various materials they were made from, and the way the pieces of the internal staircases fitted together. When it came to the towers, he knew every detail. They were built according to his design, and he loved to talk about them.

My father said, I have these two doctors' appointments.

What are the appointments for? I said. It was the first I'd heard of them. I pictured a dentist, holding a small circular mouth mirror, and an ophthalmologist scribbling out a prescription for new glasses.

They're just two appointments my doctor wants me to go to.

For what?

I don't know, he said. Something to do with my last CAT scan.

What CAT scan? I said. When did you have a CAT scan?

My father thought for a second. It was probably about a month ago, I guess, he said. They found some bump under my ribs, and so now they want me to go to these two appointments, to have this thing looked at.

What thing? I said.

It's nothing, my father said. It's just nothing. It was a lump. They think they felt some kind of lump or something. They don't know. They don't think it's anything. They don't know what it is. Some kind of bump. It's probably nothing. They just want me to go to these two other doctors now, so they set up these appointments for me, and I'm going this week. That's all.

Who are the doctors? I asked. What kind of doctors are they?

One is an internal doctor, and the one tomorrow is something else. I can't remember what kind of doctor he is.

You don't know what kind of doctor you're seeing?

I don't remember. Some kind of specialist.

Didn't your doctor explain what this was about, though?

He just sent me on these appointments, son. That's it. It's no big deal.

Okay, but did you ask the doctor what this was about? I mean, did you ask him any questions?

You know how it is, you don't even talk to the doctor anymore. I hardly even see the guy. He's my primary care physician. He just sends me to other doctors.

There was so much to say, but it was too late to get into anything.

I told my father that he should stay at the doctor's office and ask questions. Do not leave until you understand what's going on, I said. That's their job, or part of it anyway. It was all I could manage to think to say. How flimsy it seemed next to what I needed to say. They have to explain things to you, I said. They have to.

Well, maybe I'll take you with me next time, he said, and let you ask all the questions you want, and we can stay there until you understand.

I looked around my apartment, trying to locate some sign that would just tell me what to say. I could see all the rooms from where I sat, all the rooms and all my stuff inside them. I looked out the window. The parking lot of the shopping center across the street was nearly deserted. Several restaurants, a bar, a florist, a hardware store, and a grocery store I sometimes referred to as my grocery store. Yellow sodium vapor lights. A street sweeper polishing up the pavement. A couple walking toward their car.

PARABLE OF THE EXPERTS
AND THEIR WAYS

T HE ARMY of experts has advanced roughly halfway across the plains, heading east. Late last year, the experts' elite brigades, a highly trained force numbering in the hundreds at least, landed at six strategic points along the eastern seaboard. The elite brigades came ashore under cover of darkness. They wore wet suits, which they peeled each other out of upon landing. Underneath, they wore business suits, ties, shoes. They made no fires and no fuss. They hardly made any noise. They ate their food out of cans, washed the cans in the ocean, and separated their garbage into piles of that which may be recycled and that which cannot. On their persons, they carried briefcases and binders stuffed with papers. It was plain to see that the papers were of a statistical and columnar nature. They possessed supporting graphics, a series of illustrative models, various pedagogical devices, and some unverified number of laser pointers. Certainly pie charts were close at hand. According to several independent witnesses who have recently come forward, the experts mimed and gestured their way through memorized public speeches and presentations. Our best guess is that the experts undertook the performances on the beach as a final preparation before invading, simply to smooth over any minute rough spots. They studied their body language and their efficacy. They noted their overall likability and expressed it as a percentage. The laser pointers are of particular concern, because they are thought to be quite persuasive in the hands of those trained to use them.

The most recent intelligence indicates that the places where the experts landed are now irretrievably lost. The cities have fallen to their control. Our map is turning blue, as the experts make their way across the country. As our pins come out, their blue pins go in. It's a miserable business, updating the map with the pins.

Our best forward reports suggest that the elite brigades are busy, working their way west. According to sources close to the administration, the brigades traveled in a southerly direction before, but that's all changed, overnight almost. Now they're working their way west, toward us, working to make the conventional wisdom more conventional, or, in some cases, working to alter the conventional wisdom. However it suits them. It hardly matters which, really. What matters is that everything and every person they touch, they reduce to evidence, example, indicator.

Take Samantha Anne Wilson, age twenty-six, lifelong resident of Jamestown, New York, currently residing at 1405 East Avenue, apartment three. Wilson is a mother of three children, ages four, two, and six months. Wilson works in a dentist's office, doing the insurance paperwork. She enjoys making desserts, watching television, and going to the park. Wilson, or whatever is left of her now, may be best remembered as a component in certain published reports on life expectancy, infant mortality, family income as it correlates to education, et cetera, et cetera.

The experts are turning us into brittle things is the point, brittle and thin. By the summer solstice, their brigades will join the main army and combine forces. They will rally and have their way with us. We expect them to meet at approximately latitude 39°8' north, longitude 81°37' west. Such is their plan as I know it.

We lie between the two approaching camps.

I was an expert once. Or, I should say, I believed myself expert in certain areas, specifically virtual mathematics and various applied manipulations of infinity as they relate to the major stock-market indices. As some of you may know, I've since repudiated that period in my life, however, and so stand before you today a new man, decidedly and vigorously inexpert, joyously inexpert, in fact. And I stand before you to warn you and to say that this army of experts must be stopped. Moreover, we must stop them. For who else will? Now, I could stand up here and show you certain bar graphs and line charts that would horrify you, possibly anger you, perhaps even incite violence, but instead let me say this: I will help you. If you allow me to do so. Let me. Let me help you. I will do what I can. We all must. If you choose. For our efforts will require your total cooperation, of course. If you should be willing. Dedication, devotion, and commitment—you are, I trust, familiar with all these qualities? We will work together, yes? If you want? But let any one of you be unsure or even momentarily waver in the slightest, and we will most assuredly fail. How bad would that be? It would be bad, let me tell you. But don't think of that, not now. Put it out of your minds. It's all just too depressing. I get depressed. Even just speaking of it generally fills me with gloom. But look, if we work together, we will succeed. Surely, we will succeed. How could we not succeed? In the end, I mean.

Now, this is what we will do.

PRAYER FOR THE MOTHER

IMAGINE SHE IS your mother, and she is falling down the stairs. Now imagine you hear about the accident two days later, by telephone. You're told she didn't go to the hospital until late in the afternoon, the day after she fell. She just thought her arm was sore, bruised a little bit. When she finally went to the emergency room, the muscles in her arm had so seized up that the bone could not be set. Her arm could not be moved. Doctors gave her how much morphine so she wouldn't feel anything when they wrenched her arm back into place? Your father is amazed by her strength. Your mother, he says, is like a horse. A weaker person, he says, would have gone to the hospital right away. This is some of what you hear. You learn of it too late. Two days late, and you are of little use. You are three hundred and twenty-nine miles away.

PRAYER FOR THE DRIVER AT NIGHT

THE NIGHT PLAYS tricks on more than the eyes. It is nearing eleven, and he is driving. He is going to meet his girlfriend, at her parents'. As the highway goes, he is still nearly three hours away. He is late. It's nearing eleven-thirty. It is nearing midnight. It's now after twelve. The night plays tricks on more than the eyes.

HE TASTES the cheeseburger he ate four exits ago. Now he tastes fries. A cool sip of the orange-colored soda. This is not taste as in the taste is still in his mouth; it is taste like he is chewing it right now.

HE SMELLS SOMEONE he hasn't seen in more than five years. The smell in the truck is exactly how her forearm smelled once. It's not his forearm—he checks. Then he checks once more.

THE ROAD IS all physics and math. One hundred fifty-seven miles by the last sign. One hundred fifty-seven miles of 5,280 feet each. Sixty-five miles an hour. For miles now, all he's touched is the steering wheel, the gas pedal, and the back of the seat. Physics and math. He feels like a balanced equation. He is force and mass and fourteen dollars in assorted chemicals.

It's getting to be time to stop and fill up with gas. Signs say he's approaching the final exit before the turnpike.

He drags a squeegee across the windshield with one slow,

consistent motion. Looking into his truck, he sees that it's filled with a reflection of the filling station, brilliant with pure white fluorescence.

AT CERTAIN SPEEDS, with the window cracked just so, he hears sirens. The sirens come from every direction. They come from miles around. An all-points bulletin.

AND HIS EYES, of course his eyes are playing tricks on him. He hopes, anyway, that the headlight beams from the cars heading in the opposite direction are not as solid as they seem. He hopes, for what it's worth, these are just tricks. But what to make of the phantom freeways? The expansion bridges and the overpasses constructed of huge blocks of darkness. The highway interchanges and the six-lane loops made of something darker than the dark. He sees them from a mile away. They acquire detail as he gets closer. They never head in the direction he's going and then, just like that, they disappear.

Up ahead, another structure looms. This one's a bridge, some feat of demented engineering, improbable in its way, but stunning, like a thing made from spines. What drivers drive on the phantom freeways? He sees no lights. Where are they going? He sees no indication of direction. Are they alone? He doesn't even know who they are. And who constructs these phantom freeways? Who designs this nighttime road system that is not for us? Who works on the shift that pushes and manipulates and stacks and rearranges the half-ton indigo blocks of midnight that dazzle him like nothing the radio offers, and conspire to keep him driving, keep him driving, keep him driving?

PRAYER FOR A SIGN OF THE CROSS

I N DALLAS, in late August, he was shopping with his mom and dad and younger brother. He was twelve. He and his brother split off from their parents and were walking to the place that sold freshly squeezed lemonade when they passed a woman. There was nothing noteworthy about her, nothing that he can recollect, anyway. She just looked like a shopper. Nevertheless, as he and his brother walked by her, he for some reason made the sign of the cross. Now, his family was not particularly religious. They went to church, but only out of habit. They made their signs of the cross with good intentions, but also because the service called for it.

His gesture in the mall was quick and then it was over. The woman probably didn't notice. He hadn't even had time to think, I am going to cross myself. He no sooner saw the woman than his right hand moved from his forehead down to his chest across to his left shoulder and then back to his right.

He asked his brother, Did you see that?

See what? his brother said.

That woman. We just walked by her. He looked behind him but couldn't find her in the crowd.

His brother shrugged. I didn't notice anyone, he said.

Years later, when he thinks about this moment—and he will think about it, often at odd times, while checking to see that he locked the car door, for instance, or standing in line at the company cafeteria—he will think that something about the woman compelled him to make the sign of the cross. He will use that word, compelled, and it will feel right, for there is, really, no other word. And yet he'll forever be at a loss to explain how he was compelled or who it was who had compelled him.

PRAYER FOR THE SAFETY OF
THE PUBLIC SCREAMER

FROM MY WINDOW, I can see the bus shelter. A woman is walking away from it, and there's a man underneath, standing. Both are dressed in the clothes of the season, and both are angry.

The man I have seen before. I call him Screamer. I hear him before I see him. In this way he is not like a jet fighter. Today, Screamer has a splint on his nose, making it longer and more pointed. When he screams, his splint quivers. Much of what he screams is profane, curses and swears. He often screams, Asshole fall off the fucking earth.

In the mornings, I hear him coming from the west, walking toward downtown. Later, in the evenings, he returns, walking toward the suburbs. He keeps a fairly tight schedule, Screamer does. In this way he is not unlike people who work at jobs downtown. Always he is angry. Always he is screaming.

I have seen Screamer look over his shoulder, back at the suburbs in the morning or back downtown in the evening, and I wonder what to make of that looking back. My first thought was that he was being followed. Someone was after him. He had made someone angry. My second thought was that he just believes he's being followed. Whatever the case, Screamer is always yelling at the place he leaves, yelling at what he leaves behind. In this way he is not unlike you, or us, those, say, who have ever felt disappointed by the most recently passed experience, the last big letdown, that time we let ourselves think we were lucky, blessed, made from gold and promises. Precious stones never did rain on us.

Which brings me again to what I see from my window. The bus shelter. The woman walking away. Screamer standing underneath.

The woman is angry. Screamer, she thinks, screams at her. And why shouldn't she take Screamer personally? Perhaps he told her, Asshole fall off the fucking earth. The woman bends down to pick something up, and I think she's going to throw something. I think, She's going to hit Screamer. But it's just snow, and the snow is so powdery and dry, it scatters immediately after leaving her hand. She might as well have hurled a handful of dust.

And Screamer still screams. The woman's hair has come undone under her scarf, and she pauses a second to fix it. Screamer curses her, more loudly this time. Asshole, he says. Fall off the fucking earth.

The woman walks away, and then the woman comes back.

She walks to the corner, and then she comes back. This time, the woman spits at Screamer. And still, Screamer screams.

Once more the woman walks away and comes back. And once more she spits at Screamer.

As she walks away, I hear her say, I could kill you.

From my window, I see the woman crossing the street and walking along the hillside. Screamer is still at the bus shelter and still cursing. Maybe this will be the last time I see him. Maybe someone will kill him. Maybe some people will return for him and do what, I do not know. Fuck him up good.

I wish I could intervene. I want to manifest myself on the ground, between Screamer and the woman. I want to move between them. I want to say, Wait, please, you don't understand. Hold back your blows, okay? Stay, for a second, the stones you've selected for this man's skull.

And what if the woman then came upstairs to my apartment? What if she could see what I see? Look, from my window. I'm asking you. Perhaps something would come of it: me, on the ground, meeting Screamer, while she sits upstairs. With the woman may come the hundreds, maybe the thousands, of people who will ever meet Screamer outside, on the streets and on the sidewalks. They all can crowd into my apartment, jostling for a view, a seat, a spot by the window.

But can I say, really, that I wouldn't feel insulted?

Asshole fall off the fucking earth.

There is spit, and then there is the anger, like fingertips gripping my scalp.

PARABLE OF NOT SEEING

I MUST HAVE misplaced my glasses somewhere. My vision is such that without my glasses, I cannot see my glasses. Years ago, when I wasn't wearing my glasses, the pair sitting on the bureau or the nightstand or the top of the toilet still looked like glasses. They were, by me, easily spied. Last year, however, my glasses began to look like a smudge. Still, I became accustomed to this particular smudge, distinguished as it was by a bit of metal, a little reflected light. I could confidently call this smudge glasses. I perfected the ability to discern the glasses smudge from the book smudge or, yet more difficult, the loose silverware smudge.

Today, though, I was fresh out of the shower and I couldn't find my glasses. I just couldn't see the familiar smudge anywhere. It had to have been today that I lost them. I can't have been looking for more than a day.

I'm outdoors, because I'm still looking. I'm pretty certain I haven't been looking too long. I am barefoot and wearing my robe. I acquaint myself with the smudges that are cars and trucks. I know their sounds, their engines and their horns. I cross two streets and head down an alley, I think. Seems like a playground up ahead. Could be a recently mowed field, I'm not sure. If I find children, perhaps I can enlist them in my cause. Children can lead me to adults, who can help me. Children are so good.

I pass a person smudge. Hello? I say. Doesn't seem to hear me. He's leaning into a pay phone as if embracing it. I overhear his conversation. But, honey, he says, I can't find them. I don't know where

I put them. I'm not playing games, honey. I'm really not. I wouldn't joke around like that. Why would I joke around?

I double back to stand behind him. I tap him on the shoulder and point at the street signs, a green cross suspended in midair. I say, Tell her I can make some of this out. I wave my hands, gesturing to every single thing that surrounds us. Tell her we're near a mailbox, a newspaper machine, and, I think, a fire hydrant. And I hear children. Tell her about the children. It might be a playground. Children can lead us to adults, and adults can help us maybe. Nearby, there's a building and, across the street, another one, darker than the first. Tell her we're at the corner of a cross.

PARABLE OF A MERCIFUL END TO DREAMS OF FIGHTING UNDERWATER

My OPPONENT always announces himself the same way. He says, I have a bum. Warning. I know he means bomb, but he pronounces it in the pinched way of the British. Bum. Warning. I have a bum. Yet he is not British. He has, in fact, never ventured outside the States. He does, however, have a bomb. That is why he's my opponent, my dear enemy.

The city is our battlefield. Streets and avenues have, for me, pugilistic significance, a long history of beatings and many losses. You may walk past these sites without knowing it. I have met my opponent in fields, in parks, in city squares. He has met me onboard buses, subways, and monorails. We have fought under overpasses and over rivers. I have struggled against him amidst the carnivals of summer. He has found me cowering in the beverage aisle of a grocery store, hiding in the shadow of a pyramid of Coca-Cola. In tropical restaurants, cool rooms, windy vistas, snowy heights, there is, we believe, no place we haven't already fought. Were you unwittingly in attendance at some of our more celebrated bouts? We have wrestled atop buildings, decorating the skyline like two feisty hood ornaments. Always the game is simple, as my opponent takes pains to point out: one fall, mano a mano, me or the man with the bomb.

When I fight, however, I am at an immediate disadvantage. When I try to punch him, there's no force behind it. I draw back my arm, but that's it; that's all I have time for. When I try to run, I escape from nothing. I am always caught in midturn, pivoting and pushing off with my strong foot, but no more. Caught and then hit and then hit again, I fall. There is something in me that works against the punch, against my flight; it subverts each of my attempts. It is like misdirection. It is like the fact that water is at its thickest, its most dense, seconds before freezing. It, I say, because it hasn't any name. It is all effect and no identity. In my most productive moments I come up with descriptions of it; I test them against my experience, comparing them against my bruises, measuring them alongside my memories of the man standing over me and laying into my body with whatever happened to be handy—a socket wrench, a golf club, a tire iron, a stick. It is like second-guessing raised to the power of ten. It is like an interior monologue as loud as a rock concert. It is like the flashlights of a hundred righteous accusers. Everything I do, anything I try, whatever I can manage, it is in double slo-mo. This is the cruelty of fighting underwater.

Do I even need to tell you that my opponent is not similarly afflicted?

Other opponents trade in casual menace. They like to say, I've been watching you, or, I know where you live. My opponent says, I know what you feel. He describes my small, daily failures to me. As if I didn't know. His assessments are pinches that leave marks on the inside of my skin. He tells me, You are the Neville Chamberlain of your extended family. Or he says, Your love is like the plastic cups left over from a party. My body serves up for him a set of ready metaphors. Your stomach is a growing pit, he says, down which fall the snakes of your seven indiscretions. They are like arrows, their heads like arrowheads, and they move, constantly, one over another. Are you feeling that? he says. When I don't answer, he asks, Don't you understand?

I'm not sure, I say. Then, after some thought, No, not really, I guess.

112

I'm talking about your insignificance, he says, as if it could all be so plain.

I get what you're saying, I tell him. In general, I mean, but you lose me on the specifics most of the time.

My opponent actually looks sort of hurt. Should I be less gnomic or something? he says.

I shrug. It would, I guess, be a start.

Consider arrows, he says, speaking more slowly this time. Arrows in an empty stomach.

Now do you see why I fight him? Even though my moves are slow? My efforts futile? I fight him because I must. I have no other choice, I think.

When I'm not fighting my opponent, I see other people whom I imagine are fighting their opponents, on other nights, in distant parts of a darkened globe. Between dinner and dawn, the city is turned over to these fights. A long fight card every night. Many matches and many falls. Who are these people? How can you recognize them? They are those who misbutton an article of clothing. They are those who react last and late to a joke. We are the people whom you find always looking down and seemingly in. Eye contact is for the foolish when it is night and an opponent is about. We stumble frequently, unfazed. We step into traffic, neither surprised nor frightened when we realize our mistake. Not a day goes by that we do not find ourselves stopping people like you and asking for directions in the city of our birth.

PRAYER FOR THE LONG LIFE OF
CERTAIN INANIMATE OBJECTS

THE NEW ROBOT crouched on a platform beside the baby's crib and watched over the child. It cared for him. It also completed various chores, folding and unfolding the baby's blanket, for instance, as well as raising and lowering the shades in the baby's room. The robot fetched things, too. In the kitchen, it stood at the counter, heating bottles on the stove and warming up baby food. After meals, it brought a damp paper towel to the table, to wipe the baby's face and hands. When the child needed changing, the robot pinched the ends of his diaper together while the mother fastened the safety pins.

Later, in a series of family photos, the child stood between his father and the robot. His father had an arm around his mother's waist and a hand on top of his head, and through all of this posing, while they kept their smiles fixed and listened for the sound of the shutter, he had to hold hands with the new robot. His father told him to.

His mother said she thought it would look cute. To his mother, everything looked cute. Birds were cute. Dogs were cute. Babies, of course babies were cute. He could come indoors with mud clods stuck to the soles of his shoes and grass in his hair, and he looked cute. Dressed for church in a tie that made his neck throb and shoes that pinched his feet, he was too cute. Sometimes adorable, sometimes like a little man.

You're almost as tall as the robot, his mother pointed out. The robot squeezed his hand slightly. It didn't hurt. It just felt like holding hands with a robot. He took his hand back and held hands with himself instead. His father said he ruined several pictures by not holding hands with the robot. Why didn't he listen? his father asked. Why didn't he do as he was told?

His mother eased herself into a chair and sighed. She crossed her hands over her belly. His brother, on his way. You should listen to your father, she said. You're only making things worse for yourself.

His father fiddled with the camera a bit. He ran his fingers through his hair. One more picture, he said. Okay?

What he held hands with—what he was supposed to hold hands with—was a heavy, stainless steel, two-pronged claw. Its plastic fingertips felt soft to the touch, nubby, like the rubber thimbles secretaries use to riffle through papers. Wires encircled the robot's wrists and ran up the inside of its arms, disappearing into what would, on a person, be armpits, but which the father called ports. That's when the boy cried, because he didn't like to hold hands with the robot and never did, even for a family photo. Maybe even especially for a family photo. Yes, especially.

THE TWO BROTHERS were arguing over whose turn it was to use the magnifying glass. They liked the magnifying glass, which came in a black case lined with green felt. Because there seemed not enough time in the day for either brother to employ the magnifying glass or because there were too many things to magnify, they fought to control it. They had no choice. They sat in the den, on the carpet, with their backs against the couch. Beside them, a window looked out onto the backyard. They argued about who had the magnifying glass last, and then they argued over who had something that most urgently needed magnification. The older brother presented the hind leg of a grasshopper. The younger brother countered, ineffectively, with the callus on his hand. It's all dry and stuff, he said. He pointed to his palm and flicked the callus back and forth. It's ready to come off.

Questions about the magnifying glass were important. If only they could determine once and for all who had it last, everything clsc would fall into line, and the argument would end. Grasshoppers and katydids jumped out of the yard and hit the window periodically, bouncing off. From inside the den, this sounded like someone tapping to get their attention. The brothers stopped arguing at the sound, looked around, then went back to arguing. The magnifying glass lay on the carpet between them.

This was around about when their father walked into the den. The brothers were in the midst of settling their argument and starting a new, related argument. When the older brother saw the father, he thought, Finally, father has come. He'll end this argument, and he'll give me the magnifying glass.

The younger brother thought, Father likes me better.

Either of you boys seen the remote to the new robot?

They hadn't seen any remote. They shrugged and glanced around at places they plainly knew the remote wouldn't be. They didn't see any remote.

Can't remember where I was when I last used it, the father said.

The brothers couldn't care less. They didn't much like the robot. Who could say if they even liked their father. He had his moments, they guessed. Building the robot had consumed him, and then he devoted himself to operating, programming, and maintaining it. He spent hours at such work, days, mostly alone in his office, soldering colored wires and delicate capacitors to circuit boards. He chewed the end of his tongue while he worked and sweated through his undershirt until broad wings spread from beneath his arms and across his back.

When their father was working on the robot, he was not to be disturbed. Noise at his door, however slight, broke his concentration and brought him to his feet. Most of the time, when he finished work for the day, he invited his sons to look at what he'd done, but they could not touch. They could never touch. One day, the robot ever so slowly raised its arm above its head. Another day, it gripped a pencil. The father frittered away a weekend training the robot to grip and then snap a pencil.

Outside, and on their own, the brothers played robot. The older brother pretended his hand was a remote, his fingers levers, his palm lined with rows of buttons. Raise your left arm, he said. His younger brother whirred and buzzed and spun around. Raise your left arm, the older brother said, louder this time. The robot never worked properly, that was the essence of the game. His brother stopped spinning. Slowly, as slowly as the real robot, he raised his right arm and then crossed his eyes. The older brother looked at his hand, studying the controls. Then, he looked at his brother. His tongue was lolling from the side of his mouth. The robot never did as it was told.

Questions about what something electronic was or how it worked drew puzzling answers from their father. His explanations began simply enough, but soon wandered into a thicket of half thoughts, difficult words, and obtuse gestures, none of which he could ever be bothered to clarify. Once, the father cupped a fist in his hand and began to flap his elbows up and down. He looked at his sons then and raised his eyebrows, fully expecting this mechanical demonstration to enlighten them. He concluded his lessons in haste, usually in some unsatisfying way, with the sort of artless summation that passes for careful instruction. That's just the way things are, the father said. He smiled at his older son and patted the head of his younger.

The father looked around the den, but still couldn't find the remote. He lifted his hands from his sides and then dropped them, as if they had proven too heavy. How about you both help me look for that remote then? he said. How does that sound?

Arguing over the magnifying glass sounded a good deal better to the brothers, but they started to look anyway. The father turned to leave, to look somewhere else, and the older son formed his face into a version of his father's. He let his jaw go slack and left his mouth hanging open, as if he, like his father, were too distracted to remember to shut it. Lowering his forehead over his eyes, to hood them, added to the overall accuracy of his impersonation. The older son tucked his chin to his chest then and followed after his father. He let his pelvis lead him. This is what it's like, he thought, to walk like father walks. The younger brother pushed the magnifying glass underneath the couch with his foot, planning to circle back for it later.

AT LEAST THE ROBOT couldn't manage calculus. The robot managed everything else and did so handily, but it could not even begin to understand calculus. Differential equations made its processors overheat, which placed a burden on the primary cooling fan, which drew power away from the small servomotors, which rendered the robot all but useless, immobile, paralyzed.

One day, the brothers got home from school and found their father bent over the robot. The younger brother was in the sixth grade. He had projects to do and book reports. In his best projects, wars had winners and leaders exhibited uncommon valor. Everything could be conveyed by pasting cutouts and maps to half a poster board and then, as the teacher and his peers looked on, reciting a brief book report. The older brother was in the ninth grade. His favorite class was precalculus, because it was so ridiculously easy for him. And because he had learned to master something that taxed the robot. He was better than the robot, smarter and more capable, of a higher order, even. Calculus homework was like a video game: complete whatever absurd set of challenges they throw at you, then advance to the next level. He played games with a serious face and went about his work efficiently and without cheer.

The father had flipped open the back of the robot and let the first layer of innards dangle from dozens of wires. Parts lay scattered all over a bedsheet printed with lambs driving cars. The bedsheet had once been the younger brother's favorite, and for the first time he felt a hollowness whose bottom could not be plumbed, a feeling he learned later to call nostalgia. Their father had his head stuck inside the robot. He was fiddling around, twisting something or other. Then he snapped a new chip into the main board, turned it over to solder the contact points, and finally stood. He stretched his back and grunted, sounding satisfied, as if he'd just consumed a well-made meal. When he saw that his sons were there, watching him, he looked surprised. He hadn't realized it was time for them to be home already. Had they only had a half day at school?

They wished.

Was it later than he imagined? He looked out the window and tried to judge by the sun, but he wasn't sure he could tell anything from the sun. He looked back at his boys instead and smiled. Your father, he said, has just solved the problem of our robot not being able to handle calculus.

The father turned the robot on and it rotated once around its central axis. Then it reversed directions and rotated in the opposite direction. Next, it raised one arm and, ever so slowly, lowered it again, before going through the same motions with the other arm. The robot performed these actions whenever it first came on. It was some kind of diagnostic routine, this herky-jerky dance, and it lasted for several minutes. The brothers found it really annoying. The younger brother sometimes performed the routine before cleaning his room or doing his chores.

THE WHOLE FAMILY seldom sat down for dinner together. They rarely had the chance. Though they made numerous plans and talked about it and coordinated, something usually came up. At the last minute, as pots on the stove simmered for too long, the phone rang. It was the older brother again, calling to say he was at his girlfriend's. They were going to a movie, he'd be home later, so he couldn't make it, unfortunately, as it turned out, and wanted to apologize. See you, he said.

One time, however, they all managed to sit down and have their dinner together just how they planned. They passed bowls of peas and corn around the table. Mashed potatoes made the rounds. Slices of ham. Generous helpings of garden salad from a heavy hickory bowl that stayed in the center of the table. Choices of several dressings, even.

The house was full of their noise, good noise, the noise of a bunch of people living and eating and talking, contributing their jokes and laughter, the news from the front lines of their days. The father told a story about when he was young and had just begun to date their mother. They were at a beach in New Jersey with friends, and had found a piece of driftwood almost as long as their car. It was a drift log, really, the father said. He looked at their mother, and she nodded.

It was like a drift tree, she said. It was pretty big as driftwood goes.

We had this idea, though, the father said, that we wanted to take it back with us, as a keepsake.

It was quite large as keepsakes go, their mother said.

We thought we'd trade it back and forth, the father said. Neither son had heard this story before. Neither had really heard their parents talk this way. They didn't dare interrupt.

Somehow we got it in the car, the mother said.

I thought we strapped it to the top of the car, the father said.

We tried, the mother said, but we had no rope, remember? Nobody around had any rope. The father nodded. He was trying to remember, trying to picture the piece of wood. In the end, it fit inside the car, their mother said. It went right up against the windshield and stuck out the back, over the backseat.

The father smiled to hear her talk, to think of that time. This was when your father drove the convertible, he said.

Your father was very proud of his convertible.

I was, wasn't I? he said.

When they were done with dinner, when they'd all eaten what they could, nobody moved to get up. Nobody had to be anywhere, or if they did, they didn't say. They were full, yes, but also satisfied. There was a spell over the table, a blessing. How else to account for their joy? They all could sense it, even the father. They were full. They were satisfied. They wanted to remain there forever if they could.

The older brother made silent promises he knew he probably wouldn't keep, vows so crazy they could only be thought. We'll eat every meal together, as a family. As a unit. We could grow old. We could all become fat and frail and tell ourselves, This is life. This is love. These are our bodies. This is our love. The older brother looked around the table, at his parents and brother, and felt his chest might split open. His eyes teared up and then he laughed, just to let the pressure off. Nobody asked what in the world he was laughing at, and nobody looked confused. They knew.

Meanwhile, in the kitchen, in a corner, in the dark, the robot squatted between the pantry and the oven. It was caught on the pantry door and confused by the residual heat from the oven. The robot's clock blinked the incorrect time. 12:00, the clock read. The robot could not move. Its motor spun in vain, making an angry, high-pitched mechanical squeal. Then the gearbox reversed directions, and the motor spun again. The robot was stuck. It absently rubbed one of its arms against the side of the counter. There was nothing for it to grip. Someone had left a pot holder on top of its head. 12:01, the clock read. It was stuck good this time. 12:02.

IT WASN'T UNTIL the younger brother left home for college that his parents discovered what masters they were at getting on each other's last nerve. Father and mother became husband and wife, and neither knew what to make of that, frankly. It was like trying on old clothes and wondering, I actually bought this outfit? I wore it? It was me?

The husband withdrew to his office. He was working on plans for a small, nimble robot, something he called a wall-climber. Nothing workable ever came of it, but for months he saw it fully realized in his dreams. It hung from imaginary ceilings. It changed light bulbs that were hard to reach and wholly hypothetical. He was not consumed by his work; he fed himself to it.

His wife wanted to get out more. She wanted to drive to places written up in magazines. Old houses, mansions recently opened to the public, a cave where an underground lake was discovered. She also wanted to square-dance. A flyer tacked up on a bulletin board at the grocery store had caught her eye. Want to dance? it read. Yes, she thought. I suppose I do. She hadn't considered dancing as some big missing piece in her life, and she hadn't given square dancing a thought since junior high gym, when what was her partner's name again? Timothy Reynolds. Timothy Reynolds, with his sweaty hands and his BO. Once asked, however, she found she wanted to dance as often as possible.

She got involved with a semicompetitive but thoroughly friendly group of people who danced most weekends. They swung their partners in Marriotts and do-si-doed in Holiday Inns. She loved it.

Her husband thought square-dancing was a mystery best left unsolved. He went along and at first he danced with his wife, trying best to follow her lead. But then he started to sit a few dances out and let her dance with the other men. Later, he brought a book and read while she danced. He liked reading about the future, predictions and forecasts, the way things would one day be. Only occasionally did he look up to find her in the crowd of bowing and curtsying bodies. He smiled at her, nodding her way, and then got back to his book. My wife, he thought. A bright pin in a box of nails. He preferred the sidelines, the margins, the edges of the room. He leaned his chair back against the wall. From where he sat, he could almost enjoy these dances.

Once, while they were driving to a competition outside Baltimore, the husband asked, Would it be all right if I just stayed in the car?

His wife turned into the parking lot and found an open space. She always drove.

I can just wait for you here, he said. Okay?

His wife looked through the windshield at a little crepe myrtle, one, maybe two years old. Four stakes were driven into the ground around it. Wires ran from the stakes and wrapped the trunk. Such a thin tree, no thicker than her wrist, and yet so many tiny leaves. Are they called trunks still, when the trees are so thin?

That's fine, she said. Whatever you want is fine by me.

She started to get out of the car, and her husband said, Kiss? She turned, gave him his kiss, and then collected her things.

It wasn't that day or that night or even that week or month, but not so long after the square dance outside Baltimore, the wife told her husband she was filing for divorce. Her lawyer would be in touch.

Considering how few were their assets, how inconsiderable their wealth and humble their home, the proceedings were ugly and interminable, like a long war fought for a small island. The wife made one concession to spite. She demanded to receive the robot in the settlement. True, her lawyer goaded her a bit. He thought it'd be hilarious, so much sport. A robot, in a settlement! Definitely a personal first. He'd drink and dine on the details for sure.

The wife had rejected the lawyer's idea, at least initially. It was simply too mean. She didn't want to get so punitive, she said. If that's the right word. But the more she thought about taking the robot, about using it as an end table or leaving it in the garden, for the birds to crap on, the more the idea took hold and felt oddly and perfectly just.

The husband's lawyer argued with her lawyer while she and her husband sat across from each other, saying hardly a word. The office seemed freshly unwrapped. The chairs were, of course, comfortable and silent. The table gleamed like a mirror polished for the ceiling's vanity. Their lawyers went back and forth. They were so tireless, and how they loved to talk. She could get lost in their language and almost forget she was more than a spectator at a play starring two well-dressed men.

Then the robot was hers. Her husband said, Fine. Whatever. Okay. Okay. Okay.

Just like that, the meeting was over, adjourned, whatever they call it, and she was standing on her feet, and her lawyer was shaking her hand, and somehow her hand was shaking his back. Congratulations, her lawyer said. Thank you, she said. Then: Is that the right thing to say, thank you?

THE FATHER gave his younger son the so-called nickel tour of his new apartment. This is the kitchen, the den, bathroom of course, and this is where I sleep at night, he said. Pretty self-explanatory, I suppose. The walls were bare, unpainted, and the furniture came from a rental store. Except for the desk, which looked like a child's, junior's starter desk. The father had assembled it from a kit, with an Allen wrench, a few beers, and a long night.

His son stood in the hallway, beside the thermostat, and looked around. From that point, he could almost see all the rooms at the same time. He told his father that the apartment suited him. It plainly did not.

Boxes were stacked three or four high in places against several walls. So many things, so much he had no place for. It's temporary, the father said. His son didn't know whether he meant the boxes or the apartment in general. It'll do, his father said.

The lower half of a robot lay across the kitchen table. Its torso rested in a chair, and wires dangled to the floor. Even money whether it was coming apart or getting put back together.

That's my new baby, the father said.

His son nodded and took a step toward it, as vague a show of interest as he might register.

Since my first robot, the father said, there've been a lot of advances. You remember my first robot, don't you?

His son nodded and said of course he remembered it. How could he not?

For one thing, the father said, motors have gotten so much smaller.

Batteries are lighter, more compact, and they last longer. And micro-processors, of course, the microprocessors they have today are just amazing. Well, the father said, I could go on.

His son asked what this robot's deal was anyway. His question came out as a challenge, with a thin strip of curiosity flapping behind it, like a kite's tail.

Much better movement, the father said. Both in terms of a range of motion and in terms of a diverse series of environments. Also, I've given this guy a more open-ended user interface. He's friend-lier, and totally programmable on the front end. The father was counting items off on his fingers. He bent them back and studied his hands while he talked. His son feared he was working his way to ten.

The father looked around him and frowned. Conversation was a mystery to him. He often didn't know what to say next to people. To his sons. To friends. Whomever. Before he got married, the father was afraid he and his hypothetical wife would have nothing to talk about, that there would be silences he knew not how to fill.

We should go meet this guy Bynner, he said. My new friend, I guess you'd call him. He wanted me to bring you by. I told him you were visiting.

His son patted his pockets for keys and wallet. Sure, he said. Okay.

Bynner was another of the complex's many recently divorced residents. He lived in what was called the C zone of the complex. The father lived in F. To get to C, father and son walked down two flights of stairs and followed a breezeway out into the parking lot. Heat rose up from the pavement in thick waves, and the son was staggered by it. They entered an identical building, with an iden-tical breezeway and staircase, and then re-emerged again into the parking lot. The son lost count of how many buildings they passed through and which way they turned. The apartments, the individual units, numbered in the high thousands. Air-conditioning units mounted on windowsills exhaled hot air and dripped water into puddles. The son wondered if the puddles formed identical shapes.

Bynner welcomed them to his humble abode and offered them something to drink. He opened the fridge and peered inside. I got beer, he said. And beer. Bynner wore his hair long and combed it straight back in thick rows. A pair of sunglasses hung from his shirt, and chest hair, like dandelion fuzz, bloomed beneath his pale, pink neck.

The three men took seats and sipped on their beers. Bynner favored black leather and chrome furniture, tables with glass tops, and framed photographs of Air Force jets. He was in the Air Force, he said, once upon a time.

Bynner told the son he had big plans to set his old man up on a date. There are a lot of single women here, Bynner said. All very available. The place was just lousy with divorcées. Wall to wall.

The son said, I hadn't heard that, Mr. Bynner.

Alan, he said. Please. Call me Alan. Otherwise I'll think you're talking about my old man.

Sorry, Alan, the son said.

Anyway, Bynner said, I've been telling your old man I know how to get him some action.

That right? the son said.

All these divorced ladies are all the same, Bynner said. He settled back into the couch and rested his bottle on his stomach. Their first husbands were, to a man, louts. Just absolute louts. These guys, they didn't listen. They didn't do lady things like shop at the farmers' market or go antiquing. I mean, if you so much as ask these women what they're thinking, they dissolve into tears. Seriously. It's like being in college and the highest grade's a C minus, but there's

a generous curve, right? You got a D, and mayb
that D-student, but in this class you come out l
genius. That's what dating these women is like
are so low and they're so beaten down by life t
guy like your father, say, with a bouquet of pi
off like a real Prince Charming.

The father looked around the room. Wi
couch. He focused on a crack in the drywall. F
workmanship. How would it be to disapp
become a fly or perhaps a spider, squeezing
Then he thought, How might I build a robo
a spider for that matter? That was a true pr
plexity and one worthy of his time. He cou
it. No, weeks or months, even. The father
always had liked that phrase, lost in though
grasped and cherished it. His mind was a
forest on the edge of a new world. Given
option, he preferred to wander there.

Too bad your old man's always work
Bynner said. He gestured at the father, in
a specimen the son would do well to stud

The son said, That's what he likes, wh

I told your old man why doesn't he
said. I want me a fully automated pussy

The son looked at his father. He enj
little, his face flush.

I told him already, the father said.
construct a pussy robot. He has no ide

Hey, Bynner said, I'm just an old g

No, I'm feeling you, the son said.

Bynner swigged his beer and the

ain, as if he were a deep-swimming fish, only coming up for air. e old guy has a dream, he said. Another old guy has to come ng and kill it. That's the way of the world, sadly.

Bynner looked at the son then, hoping he might enlist him in re joking. He thrived on the stuff. Am I right? he said. Or am I t?

The son raised his bottle to him and just smiled.

The beer ran out soon enough and the talk with it. For a time, chatted about their cell phones and their calling plans, the es and minuses of them. Technology was the new weather.

ou know what? Bynner said. He paused then, for too long. It as if in the excitement of having something to say, he had for-n just to keep speaking.

e should go and look at my car, he said, finally. He clapped his s on his legs and rose to his feet. Your old man tell you about ar?

e son shook his head.

ell, it's a beauty, Bynner said.

re is, the father said. He saw their visit stretching on now for t another hour. Maybe more. Why couldn't visits end when t they should end? It had been a perfectly nice afternoon, ering.

ner took the father and son down to the garage. He opened or and switched the light on with a faint ta-da. The car was d large and old. It looked like the past's wildest fantasies he future. The son didn't know cars. He never got into them. aw the point, really. He'd never be able to afford the expen-es.

er asked the son what he drove, and when he told him, Byn-ked stricken. Like father, like son, he said.

ives fine, the son said. And it's dependable.

Crutches are dependable, Bynner said. Chairs are dependable. Gravity is dependable. Cars should be more than fucking dependable.

The son shrugged and looked away, and Bynner said he was just joshing. I love my car, he said. That's silly to say, I know, but it's true. I love this car. I mean, a man's got to love something.

The son said maybe he'd meet someone here. He didn't believe it, but he felt he had to say it. It was one of those things, an extorted platitude.

Bullshit, Bynner said. That's bullshit. That's dating. That's I don't know what it is. When I drive this car though, I know I feel good. I feel really, really good. It's like I'm floating. You, your dad, everyone else, you all drive. I float. I fly.

The son started laughing. I'm serious, Bynner said. I'm dead serious. When my car got dinged. He pointed at the rear panel on the driver's side, at some speck the son could not see even when he bent his head close to Bynner's. It was in the mall parking lot, and I swear I wanted to murder somebody. I shit you not. I wouldn't murder somebody over anything less than pure love. You know what I'm saying?

Bynner saw the son looking at the license plate: BG RD UN. It's supposed to be big red one, he said, but some asshole took that.

Bynner put the top down and checked the car over, like a pilot preparing before his flight. Only then did they all go for a spin.

While he drove, Bynner laughed. The car, the whole idea of it, just tickled him to no end. The father looked around at people they passed. A woman carrying groceries. A kid on a bike with his friend perched on the handlebars. Was everyone carrying something somewhere? His eyes began to water from the wind, so he shielded them with his hand. When that didn't help, he shut them and listened to the engine and to the road. He thought of tiny robots, each no bigger than a shirt button, and imagined holding a whole family of them in his hand.

His son spread his arms across the back seat. A person could go to sleep back here, he said.

Bynner turned around. What's that?

It's like a bed, the son said. He slapped the seat.

What? Bynner asked.

It's nice, the son said. It's a beauty.

Bynner grinned and nodded and turned back to the road. He couldn't hear a thing. He started talking and was gesturing at the car, jabbing his finger at its various features. He was saying something about the engine or maybe the dashboard, but the wind crumpled his words and tossed them away.

THE OLDER BROTHER announced he was getting married. His father got on the phone and said, I should come visit you two. I should take you out to dinner or something.

His son said he didn't have to do that. It sounded like a lot of trouble, what with the cost of a plane ticket and then going out to eat.

We should go to a nice place, his father said. Pick a place you wouldn't ordinarily go. Real top of the line, okay?

The son and his fiancée made a reservation at some restaurant they'd heard good things about, and the son began to dread the evening. His fiancée lay in bed and he rested his head on her stomach. I don't want to sound like an ingrate, he said. That was how he prefaced his most ungracious thoughts. But I just don't want him to make a fuss. His fusses are embarrassing. They're awkward. He's awkward. The son turned away and looked down the length of the bed. Dresser, plant stand, window. Jesus, he said. I feel like I'm in junior high. Don't want to be seen with my dad. Don't want to do anything together. Just want to be left alone. Blah blah blah.

His fiancée traced his ear and then rubbed his neck in a lazy way. It's just dinner, she said. We have to eat anyway.

The other day, the son said, I remembered this time my brother and I were stuck inside one of his robots. We were small. I was six, maybe seven, so my brother, he must have been four. Anyway, my father was building one of his robots, and this thing was huge. The body of it, not including the wheels or the head, was as big around as one of those metal trash cans. And it was probably almost two trash cans tall, if you can picture that.

Sounds enormous, his fiancée said.

It was his biggest robot, the son said. By far. Anyway, my brother and I wanted to see what dear old Dad was up to.

How many robots did your father have?

Maybe a dozen. I don't know. Maybe more. He had at least a dozen unique robots, but then he used those for parts, to make more robots.

Our father was in a good mood that day. You could tell. He was humming away. He hummed songs I'd never heard before. Maybe they weren't even songs. They were kind of aimless. Anyway, I wanted to see inside the robot, so my father lifted me up and put me inside. It was empty, just the shell. Then my brother of course wanted in, so my father lifted him and put him in beside me. The shell was pretty boring and dark. It looked much neater from the outside. Inside, it really was like a trash can, and we couldn't see anything. So I said I wanted out. I was bored. My father leaned over the edge of the shell and started laughing. Look at you two, he said. I got to get a picture of this. He went away. I heard him laughing and then nothing. I tried to climb out but there was nothing to grab onto. My brother just stood there all quiet-like, but I was upset. I started to yell and then I started to cry and then I kicked the side of the robot. I kicked the robot as hard as I could, repeatedly. Then I hit it with my fists, as hard as I could. But it didn't make much noise. Just this hollow thump, thump, thump. There was so little satisfaction in that sound. I hurt my feet though, and my hands.

The son lay next to his fiancée and folded his arms behind his head. Sometimes he thought it easiest to talk to the ceiling. When my father came back, my mother was with him. I guess he wanted her to see us piled into the robot. But when he heard me screaming and kicking, he lost his shit.

I can still see him staring down at us. His face was red and twisted up, like it had been dented, and a vein was running down the middle of his forehead.

Do not hit the robot, he said. Do not ever do that. Would you like it if I hit you? he asked. Would you? He started to tap me on the top of my head, lightly at first and then harder, with his whole hand. Do you like that? he said. Do you?

That's when my mother intervened, or tried to, in her usual overly nice, completely ineffective way. Honey, she said. That's not fair.

By this time my brother's crying, too. He's crying because I'm crying. But my father decides he's going to take that photograph after all. So for the next I don't know how long, he's standing over us, snapping pictures and telling us not to cry, to stop crying, crybabies.

The fiancée said, That sounds awful. She didn't know what to say. What could one say? That's just awful, she said.

The son propped himself up on his elbow. He traced figures in the bedsheets. Lines without end. A few of those pictures are in our photo albums, he said. I've seen them. My mother has them. What's weird is you'd have to scrutinize them to even guess my brother and

I are upset. It just looks like we're overheated. Maybe, you know, we're sweating, because we're in a giant trash can.

His fiancée reached for his hand. He stopped tracing and squeezed her fingers.

Do you know what I thought when I saw those pictures again?

His fiancée didn't know.

I thought maybe it didn't happen. Maybe I got it all wrong. Maybe I made it up. The whole thing. But it really did happen.

I know, his fiancée said.

It did happen, he said. The pictures are just misleading.

The son rarely felt good after unburdening himself. If something bothered him, putting it into words ruined it. Words reduced whatever troubled him to trivia. Or worse, he felt like a simp for making too much of it. Words turned against him. They never just let the bothersome thing be exactly as it was and how he remembered it.

I guess I have issues, he said. He imagined his self as a leaf floating on a sea of deprecation.

On the day of the dinner, the son and his fiancée picked his father up at the hotel. Before they could even park, his father was there. He just appeared and came bearing a gift under his arm.

He got into the backseat and hugged the fiancée from behind. Then he squeezed his son's shoulders. Hi, guys, he said.

The gift looked hastily put together. The box was torn, and the top was coming open. From the moment the son saw the gift, he hated it. Growing up, he had learned he shouldn't ever hate anything. It just wasn't proper. That's what his mother told him and his brother. If they wanted to say they strongly disliked something, well, that was okay, but they did not and should not hate, not ever. And yet, hate here was not too strong a word. As his fiancée and his father talked, wild speculation clouded the son's mind. He did not

wonder what the gift was. He knew—or at least he felt he did. The
father had brought them a robot. A goddamned robot, he thought.

Never mind that the box was on the small side. Never mind that
he and his fiancée never expressed any interest in having a robot of
their own. Never mind that the father rarely, if ever, gave one of his
robots as a present. Logic mattered not in the slightest. His mind
was galloping through unfenced fields now. Logic was but a small
stream to leap over. So against all evidence, he decided it would,
in fact, be just like his father to foist one of the robots on them, all
but insisting they incorporate it into their lives, make room for it in
their new home. The son gripped the steering wheel as if he had to
hold it in place, as if the car itself would surely fall apart were it not
for his effort to keep it together.

As it turned out, the gift was not a robot.

The father said he'd been going through some things, cleaning
his apartment, when he came across three sweaters he'd bought the
son's mother. They hadn't fit her. He'd never got her size right, not
in all their years together. Well, he was supposed to have returned
them to the store, but he put it off so long he forgot about it. And so
here they were, he said. He pressed the box into the fiancée's hands.
If you like them, and they fit, they're all yours.

The fiancée thanked the father. This is very sweet, she said. She
held each sweater up and made positive comments.

If they're not right, the father said, don't feel bad, okay? Just give
them away. Somebody will like them.

The son drove, and he tried to relax. It's just dinner. We have to
eat anyway.

Little was ever as bad as he imagined. He pictured catastrophes.
They were the stuff of his daydreams. Not explosions and car acci-
dents, but catastrophes of a personal nature. Minute insults that
got out of hand. Old grudges that grew like cancer. Still, even when

things turned out okay, the son found it hard to forget how bad they could have been. However much he tried—and he did try—he could never let dinner just be a dinner.

SOME YEARS LATER, the two brothers were cleaning out their father's apartment, deciding what they wanted to sell and what they wanted to keep, when they came across one of his old robots behind a stack of boxes in the garage. Cut-up old T-shirts that their father had used for rags were piled atop the robot.

Jesus, the older brother said.

You think it still works? the younger brother asked.

The older brother couldn't answer. Jesus, he said again.

You want it?

The older brother wasn't sure. I don't want anything, he said.

You sure? You should take what you want. Whatever you want. The younger brother pushed the rags aside and then, reconsidering, picked one rag up and began brushing the dust and dirt and grime from the robot's body.

The older brother slipped behind the robot. He crouched down and studied the back of the thing. He ran his fingers over the places where one piece came together with another, tracing its seams. He was looking for this little catch that would jimmy open the panel so that he could get at the controls. He'd know what to do once he saw it. The panel is in the back, right? he said.

The younger brother shrugged and blew at the digital display on its front. I don't remember, he said. He wet his fingers with a bit of spit and tried to polish the plastic, but the grime just smeared.

The older brother had worked a piece of metal loose and was yanking on it. He shook the robot from side to side. He was losing his hair, just a bit. The younger brother had never noticed that before. His brother's bald spot was shaped like an egg and about as large.

The younger brother knelt in front of the robot and raised one of its arms. He heard, from deep inside the robot, a motor spin. The sound was faint, a whir. It reminded him of weekend afternoons, when he was younger, of hearing that sound and seeing the robot move and then watching how pleased, even joyful, his father could be. Listen, he said. The older brother stopped what he was doing, and the younger brother lowered the robot's arm to its side. Somewhere inside, the motor reversed and then turned again. They both heard the sound. The younger brother put the robot through the same motions with the other arm. He was making the thing go. Remember how it always did that dance? he asked.

The older brother took a halfhearted stab at the impersonation they once did. God, he said, it was just endless.

The younger brother stood up and scooted behind his brother. Let me take a look, he said. He made a move. He wanted to see inside. He wanted his turn.

Will you, his older brother said, just let me do this?

You know what you're doing?

Do you know what *you're* doing?

The younger brother didn't say anything. Nobody knew what he was doing. Nobody ever did.

Still, the older brother had a purpose. He knew he did. He was just waiting for it to be revealed. Just give me a minute, he said. Okay?

The younger brother shrugged and walked off, squeezing around the back of their father's car. How much could it be worth? He stood looking out the window of the garage door. There was a time when looking out the window of any garage door seemed impossible, an unattainable goal, the province of adults. How many times had he climbed on the backs of cars just to see, stepping on their bumpers and feeling their shocks give and then push back against his weight as he turned to face a garage door and leaned against it and, finally, looked outside? There was nothing outside now, nothing of any significance. A line of identical garages stretched as far as he could see. A speckled bird, its natural coloring looking like the symptoms of a fatal disease, hopped around underneath some shrubbery.

When their father died, his younger son thought he would write a eulogy that, as he phrased it, told everyone the truth. Good and bad. The father's innumerable and tender quirks as well as his sullenness, the dark moods and unpredictable outbursts. Not just the way he collected free stuff from hotels, the pens and the paper and the tiny bottles of shampoo and conditioner. But the way he made his sons feel guilty for not using the shampoo, and cowed them into giving thanks and showing gratitude for this great overflowing bounty of hair-care products. The father had bags of the stuff. Boxes, the younger son felt sure. Probably here in the garage.

The younger son had thought he would hold nothing back, consider nobody's feelings save his own. Fuck politeness. Politeness meant being unfailingly kind to others at his expense. Had he not been polite enough for long enough? For years, he had written such incredible eulogies in his head, unsparing and forceful speeches that he delivered in the dark, in his bed, while trying to get some sleep. Coming home to visit his father often prompted him to draft a new eulogy, more up-to-date, more thorough.

In the end, he settled for something vague, and he croaked out every word. It wasn't polite necessarily, just vaguely worded generalities. It was fine. So many people, people he didn't even know, came up to him and gripped his arm or patted his shoulder and told him how beautiful was the speech he gave.

How's it coming? the younger brother asked, still staring out the

139

window. He wanted to get on with the cleaning. He wanted to finish up, just get it all done.

It's coming, his brother said.

It's coming, the younger brother said, imitating him.

His brother ignored him. He was fiddling around, twisting something or other. The insides of the robot were dense with colored wires and stacked layers of silicon boards. It was more complex than he remembered, more complex than he ever knew. How much time had his father spent on this thing? How many hours? And how many days?

I wouldn't mind finishing up, is the thing, the younger brother said.

Should just be another second, his brother said.

Another second until what?

A few minutes later, the older brother was still at it, whatever that was, up to his elbows in the robot. He worked in silence, determined to understand the thing through study. He tried to be patient. He was prepared to take the whole thing apart if necessary, breaking it down to its smallest components. Perspiration dripped from his forehead. It pooled on top of the robot and mixed with the grime. He could understand nothing.

Years before, the older brother had formulated a theory about parents and their sons and daughters. The theory held that many adults behaved and carried on like kids because their parents were still alive and still around. As medical science continued to improve and life expectancy increased, those adults acted like the children they once were for an even greater portion of their life. They just never grew up. They turned into these big adult babies. Babies with jobs and cars and mortgage payments. Babies with their own families often. Babies with their own babies to raise. They were, in some sense, stunted. Centuries ago, you'd inherit whatever there was to inherit and then you had to make your way. Maybe you got nothing. Maybe you got an old milk cow or a dinky cottage and a patch of fenced-in mud. You were sixteen or seventeen, if that. Maybe you were twenty or twenty-three, but the point was you began your life then. The older brother remembered this theory coming to him like a fist from the sky. The truth of it knocked him to his knees. No, he didn't wish his parents dead. He never wished his mother and father dead. But still, but still, why did he have to wait so long in order to live?

The older brother removed a piece of the robot and then looked at what was left. Every part that came off revealed something new. The thing was like a cake of one thousand layers. He didn't know if his theory still held true. He couldn't tell anymore whether it was right or wrong, but he was starting to have his doubts. Even if it were true, wasn't there a larger truth anyway? And an even bigger fist? And wasn't his theory too abstract? It was practically bloodless. It occurred to the older brother then that no one who had lost a parent would ever formulate such a crap theory as his.

I think I'd like to be getting out of here pretty soon, the younger brother said.

You can go, his brother said. Just go if you want to go.

The younger brother leaned back against their father's car and looked around. All this stuff. They'd have to sell the car, he supposed. Maybe they knew someone who needed a car. Somebody always needed a car. But then there were the tools, the workbench, all the projects left undone. Were the projects trash now? Did he and his brother just throw them away? Could they do that? He thought about these tasks—all this work yet to be completed—not as a practical concern (could they throw this stuff away today?) or a legal matter (were they allowed to throw the stuff away?), but rather as a crucial test of what they were capable of doing, what they were together, the two brothers, able to manage. He decided they were capable of much. It amazed him. He wouldn't have guessed it. They would, he knew, be there much longer. For them there would be no finishing up, not today anyway.

The older brother looked up from his work on the robot, surprised to see his brother still there. I said you could go, he told him. I can take care of the rest myself.

The younger brother shrugged. I'm not doing anything, he said.

PRAYER FOR SOME OF WHAT WAS LOST

ONE HUNDRED FOURTEEN ballpoint pens, ninety-seven pencils, thirty-five felt-tips, and at least six special pens, the expensive kind, gifts from behind locked counters.

Twenty-three plain white buttons, forty faux tortoise-shell buttons, and one small chrome-plated deer, leaping, which hung from the zipper of his coat in the seventh grade, until he decided to carry it around like a charm, for good luck. He kept the deer in his pocket. He liked to cup it in his hand while he walked. For a day, or maybe two days, he held on to it, and then he lost it.

In Texas, in the summer, he lost one of his pet hermit crabs for two hours, on account of falling asleep. He found it under his dresser, behind an old game he and his brother bought at a garage sale. The game had these small discs that they slid up one half of the board, angled off a couple of taut rubber bands, and ricocheted down the other side.

Later, the same pet crab would latch onto his hand. His parents had thrown a party, some kind of get-together that filled the living room like smoke. He cut his way through the gathering to get to the kitchen and pour himself a glass of limeade, then drifted back around the fringes, watching. He was trying to be unobtrusive, when a man and woman noticed him and remarked on how big he had grown, how the last time they saw him he was this small. The woman was on the sofa, and her husband was sitting sideways, perched on the arm. The husband held his hands out in front of him, as if to squeeze a loaf of bread. That small, he said.

The woman said, My husband and I go way back with your

parents, and when I say way back, I mean way back. As she spoke, she leaned away from him, sinking deeper into the sofa, until her husband caught her by the hand and pulled her upright.

He told the man and woman that he had some things to do and went to his room. Not an hour later, he ran into the middle of the party, screaming and bawling and carrying on. The pet crab was attached to his hand. He was just holding it, he said, in his palm, and it was walking around, when all of a sudden it grabbed his finger and now it wouldn't let go.

Someone suggested prying it free with a pair of pliers.

No, he said, don't, please. Everyone waited around, staring at him and looking down at the crab. They let float a few other ideas. Could he slide it off, with kind of a shimmy? No, it was really on there, and jostling the crab only made it tighten its grip. What about cold water? Cold water had, it turned out, no effect. Never a dull moment, someone said, with kids around. The crab eventually relaxed its claw, and he grabbed it up by the shell and took it back to its cage. His mother brought him a baggie full of ice and told him to lie down and stay out of trouble. His finger throbbed. Every now and then, he peeked underneath the ice. For several hours his skin retained the memory of being pinched.

It's fashionable to say so-and-so lost his childhood, but that's not how he feels. He once maintained that he had lost the places where he lived, his memories of the character of the air and an encyclopedia-like grasp of all the important street names, phone numbers, shortcuts, and hangouts. But he's not sure now what all that means. Did the places where he lived really have distinct types of air? He thinks not. Anyway, those places are in no way lost, not really. He remembers them well enough. Less and less, true, but still. They're hardly gone, not completely.

He did lose the reasons for what he did. Why, for instance, did he hide from his father when he and a neighbor girl were tossing a tennis ball in the front yard? She had just thrown him the ball, and he dove to catch it. Then his father pulled into the driveway, and he hid, just like that. He hid really ineffectively, too, leaping over a flower bed and some scraggly bushes and then crouching behind a brick pillar hardly wider than his body.

The neighbor girl came over to his hiding spot. What is it? she said. What's wrong?

Nothing, he said, I'm just hiding, you know?

Why?

He didn't have an explanation. It's like a game, he said.

Years later, when the old parish priest asked if he wanted to light the candles during mass, why did he say no, right to the priest, with his parents there?

And why did he pull a knife on his brother and lunge at him, his bed in between them? His memories lack motive; it's been washed out, or lost. He might as well be watching a TV mystery about someone whom he vaguely resembled.

Why did he steal a fishing bob from the five-and-dime? It was made of foam, or maybe cork, and painted iridescent orange and yellow. He'd never seen such a bob. The ones his family used were red and white and made of plastic. Later that day, he rode his bike to a part of the neighborhood where he'd never been. The grass was high there. The streets were paved and there were street signs and electrical boxes in the ground but no houses. Trees weren't yet cleared. That was how the land looked before they came, minus the street signs, of course, and the electrical boxes. He chucked the fishing bob down a storm sewer and pedaled home fast.

In the fifth grade, as his family was preparing to move, he spent three months sitting out recess. He just stopped playing. He walked as far from the school as he could without being considered truant and sat against a chain-link fence. He doesn't know why. He pulled a tall weed out of the ground and threw it like a spear. Then he pulled another. Even his best answers are inventions, though sometimes those inventions can be almost clever. Friends came to visit him, out by the fence, but he could hardly speak. He didn't have words. He and his friends pulled more weeds, threw more spears.

Once, he told a friend that he liked to play a game before waking. In the minutes before day, just after the first alarm rang, he kept his eyes shut and imagined all the bedrooms that were ever his. He pictured the light leaking through the windows. How did the light fall there? How was the furniture arranged? Which direction did he face? The thing is, he doesn't remember playing that game. Most likely, it was another invention, a fancy, something that sounded poignant. Unless he remembered then and has forgotten now. It's hard to say, really.

A pocketknife, a fishing lure, a flashlight. A wheat penny, a bunch of stamps, a coffee cup: lost. He got the signatures of dozens of professional golfers on a souvenir program and then dropped it into the bottom of a port-a-john. As he stared down at it, flies hovered around the seat, circling. He came outside and told his father what had happened. It was an accident, he said. It was under his arm and then he dropped it. He hadn't meant to.

Which port-a-john was it? his father asked.

He showed him, and his father looked inside. It's ruined, he said. I'm sorry.

A wristwatch with a busted band that he insisted on wearing, dropped somewhere at Houston Intercontinental. He didn't realize it was gone until a stranger approached and asked him for the time. He pawed at his wrist, bare, and then looked at the stranger. My watch, he said. For the first time, he could picture the expression on his face. He could see it in how the stranger looked at him, how his shock was reflected back as confusion, cut with a bit of sympathy. He deserved, though, to lose that watch. He should have repaired the band weeks before, maybe even months.

Keys to padlocks, combinations to bike locks, passwords, and PIN codes.

How many footraces? How many relay races, three-legged races, potato-sack races, bear-crawl races, crab-walk races? How many contests, competitions, spelling bees, science fairs, and juried exhibitions all lost?

His eyesight, he's still losing that, too.

Nickels, dimes, quarters, and pennies lost. Change dropped. Dollars stuck together. A five fixed to the backside of a one.

And what of the minutes which become hours and which then become the days and nights of squandered time, mislaid time, time spent at misadventures and asinine pursuits? This is in memory of that lost time.

Lists were lost, too, lists for groceries and errands, ambitious abbreviations of what was done and what remained still to do.

He lost his grandfathers and his grandmother, his mom's mom, who swam in the mornings and did crossword puzzles. All he has are the stray details. His grandmother brought a dictionary with her when she visited them and had an antenna on top of her house that you could make rotate with the turn of a dial downstairs. These are memory's leftovers, fragments, a couple of thoughts that don't follow. He lost his uncle, his father's brother, whom he didn't know well, not as an adult, at least. They saw *Star Wars* together, the original. He and his brother always wanted to caddie for him, because he could golf. He really knew how. He just smacked the ball. His wife's grandfather, whom he didn't get to know, because the man was losing his memory already and happiest to relive his college years. He had come into the picture too late. That's what he always thought. And then his wife's grandmother, who taught him to play bridge, who passed by rapping her knuckles on the edge of the table three times and who bid aggressively for game, and who talked of time in centuries and bold strokes, as if she had different eyes than the rest of them. A cousin of his died of a heart attack while in college. A friend's father, as cool as a dad could be to high-school kids, because he played pickup basketball and got Pink Floyd albums as Christmas gifts. The father checked into a motel room and shot himself. He always imagined the motel on the outskirts of Houston, a gravel parking lot surrounded by overgrown fields, the kind flocks of migrating geese landed in, but that's just invention. He doesn't know where the motel was. He could never bring himself to ask. The woman next door to his family went suddenly. This was the woman married to the boor who talked about football constantly and once offered to get him a job operating the elevator at the Masonic temple. Anyway, once, while her husband was away, attending a funeral, the woman needed help removing her surgical sock. It was hurting her foot, she said. He went over immediately, of course. They sat at the kitchen table, and he worked the sock off her foot, talking about what, he no longer knows. She said she was okay, but he wanted to make sure. She seemed short of breath and was gripping the table, as if to steady the room. Not much later, her husband came home. He had put chocolates in his pants pocket before he left for the cemetery. In case he got hungry, he said. But now the candy had melted and made a mess. Oh dear, the woman said. You just had that suit cleaned, too. That wasn't the last time he saw the woman, but his memory has begun creeping in the direction of that tidier conclusion.

Imagine losing the same thing every day for the rest of your life. Now imagine that there's nothing you can do about it.

Once, he kept a garden, back when he had that sort of space.

He grew two varieties of tomatoes, cherry and beefsteak, as well as radishes, chinese onions, romaine lettuce, dill, carrots, and watermelon. The watermelons never really took off. They looked like cucumbers and tasted mealy. He lived on a corner lot then, with low fences. Plenty of sun, in other words, sun all day long. They live in a city now, he and his wife, in a townhouse with a small backyard dominated by a tree taller than their home. The tree may well be older than their home, or as old, who knows. For fifteen minutes a day, or maybe thirty, the plants get their sun, and then it too is gone.

PARABLE OF WOOD AND FIRE

IN THE MORNING, the man walked into the jungle to search for wood with which to build his signal fire. He picked up some sticks here and there, a fistful and no more. What logs he came upon were sodden, bad for burning.

In the afternoon, the man ate a small amount of rabbit jerky and drank cold water from a stream. His throat clenched when the water hit it, but he kept drinking. The water was good, the pain modest, fleeting.

The man took stock of the wood: three decent-sized logs and the one handful of twigs. Not nearly enough, he thought. He did have more wood somewhere, stored away inside dry caves and in some shelters he made from mud and thatch. Lately, though, he couldn't find his way back to those places.

The afternoon wore on, and the light of the day began to dim. The man noticed a log resting on some rocks. Good position, he thought, off the ground. He nudged the log with his foot—it seemed solid enough. When he turned it over, however, he saw that the underside was wet and very nearly hollowed out. Bugs crawled along its length, scattering in the light. Termites, probably. Maybe a few grubs. They followed the grooves they had bored. Termites made the man nervous. What was the aim, finally, of such industry? As for the log, it would burn, but not for long. Two to three hours only. The termites might add something to the fire— a bit of color, the occasional pop—but the man was after something else. He wanted a fire that could, with tending, last until dawn.

The man had been building his fires every day for more months and years than he could recall. He had formulated certain ideas—theories—for what made a fire a good fire. For him, it all went back to how he stacked the wood. Fire, he believed, was an expression of the wood. And so good fires were made—or, indeed, undone—in the stacking and arranging of the logs and twigs and sticks. Everything else was heat and destruction. By properly stacking the wood, by stacking it his way, the man sought to control the heat, direct it even. In grander moments, the man considered himself something of a conductor of fire.

The man came to a clearing in the jungle. The light, suddenly brighter, hurt his eyes. There was wind from the north, and there were insects, grasshoppers or something, humming, always humming. The man was scanning the ground for anything useful, even twigs, when the insects fell silent. He looked up to see a peacock on the opposite side of the clearing. They slept in the trees near here and shit hard brown balls. The bird scratched in the dirt and then rose up on his claws, craning his neck. The man didn't move. He had no quarrel with the bird—no use for him either. In the beginning, the man had tried chasing the peacocks. Never caught one—only just exhausted himself. But the birds, when frightened, dropped their feathers, and the man collected those, keeping them, as some sort of reminder, he guessed. Of what, he was now no longer sure. All this happened years before.

The peacock turned and then walked into the jungle. The man followed it.

WHEN THE MAN was young still, he lived with his father in a room above a cannery. Their quarters were spare—a table, chair, and stool, and a thin mattress the father unrolled at night and stowed away each morning. The boy had two dolls, a girl doll he called Doll, and her pet dog, Dog. They had heads carved out of wood and wide grins painted on their faces, and he could make them do things. Whatever the boy thought up, they did. Doll delivered packages to Dog, and then Dog thanked her, and then Doll said, Bye-bye, Dog, and just went on her way. Or else they took walks together, around the room and under the table. Dog and Doll loved taking walks.

Days for the boy were easy mostly, even golden, but his father could be cruel. If the boy fell afoul of the rules, he got a beating. It was pretty simple. His father expected him to eat his supper, all of it. It mattered not whether the boy felt hungry, he had to finish what his father put in front of him. The boy chewed slowly, however. Tiny bites, choking each one down. His father didn't care how long the boy sat there. If eating took him hours, so be it. The boy was also expected to keep his mouth shut while he chewed. He saw some wisdom in this rule, but found it was not always possible to mind his father. He meant him no disrespect.

One night, his father made meat loaf, cooking it on a bed of pine straw for flavor. Sawdust mixed into the meat helped him make two decent meals rather than just the one.

As they ate, the father watched his son, eyeing him. Quit chomping already, he said.

The boy nodded and went back to his food.

I warned you, his father said.

The boy took smaller bites and chewed them even more slowly.

Are you an animal? his father asked.

The boy shook his head no.

Answer me, his father said. Are you an animal?

The boy gestured to his mouth, which was full, and continued to chew.

Then, tell me, his father said, why do you eat like an animal eats?

The boy finished chewing and said he was very sorry. It wouldn't happen again, he promised.

They ate in silence for a few minutes more.

The father put his fork down and looked at his son. If you're going to insist on eating like an animal, he said, you can eat downstairs.

The boy was unsure of what he had done. He thought he was doing everything right.

Go, his father said. Take your food and go.

The boy picked up his plate and his fork and his napkin.

I don't want to look at you anymore, his father said.

Downstairs, the boy walked among the cannery works, the hulking machines, the rollers, and the gleaming line. His father's family had run this cannery going back several generations. The boy found a few boxes of cans and fashioned them into a stool and a table. He thought, This isn't so bad, really. The place smelled like oil, but he could, he thought, grow accustomed.

Later, after the boy had finished eating, his father came downstairs and told him to pull his pants down, his underwear too, and then he gave him the belt good. The boy cried, and his father cried as well. The boy always thought it odd that his father cried when he hit him, but cry he did, blubbering on about how much he didn't want to have to do what he was doing, and so forth.

After, as the boy dressed, his father told him how much he loved him. Give your father a big hug, he said.

The boy looked at him.

Come on, his father said. He bent down then and held his arms open wide, and the boy did what he always did, he ran to his father.

THE PEACOCK led the man through parts of the jungle he had not seen. They walked under plants with droopy leaves larger than his head. Dragonflies hovered near and then darted away. Ferns grew tall here, like trees, almost, and gnarled vines thick as the man's wrist hung from the branches above. The man tried to move one vine aside, sweeping it with his hand as he passed, but it creaked and then the tree shuddered and the bird quickened his step. While he walked, the man collected what wood he saw. It was good stuff. A bit damp, perhaps, but solid—wood he could dry, given time.

Up ahead, the peacock entered another clearing. The man placed his wood on the ground and then crawled ahead, to the edge of the clearing, where he knelt behind a plant whose name he did not know. Peacocks, ten or twelve of them at least, moved through the grass. Small chicks scratched and pecked at the dirt. There were male birds and female birds both. Maybe there were more than twelve. It was hard to count them all. The man thought he had come upon their society. That was the word he used. It wasn't a family, he knew that much. There were simply too many birds and, anyway, too many males. A couple of the peacocks called out, emitting loud shrieks that pierced the air. The hens waddled off and then returned. The man could make no sense of any of it. It seemed at once aimless and strictly choreographed.

The man stood and stepped into the clearing. The chicks ran about, just scratching and pecking away, but the older birds froze in their places. The man walked among them, admiring them, their brilliant and improbable colors. He saw things then he had never noticed before: the wrinkled-up skin that covered their claws, and how, from behind, their feathers supported one another in many fine and overlapping layers.

The peacock that the man had followed stood near the center of the clearing. The man approached, holding his hands to his sides. I'm sorry, he said. He thought he detected a bit of movement in the bird's eyes.

I wanted to see where you were going, he said.

The peacock didn't move.

I'm gathering wood, the man said. For a fire. He gestured behind him, where he had left his woodpile. I build fires, he said.

The man showed the peacock the palms of his hands. I'm not here to hurt you, he said.

The chicks ran around his feet.

The man started back toward his woodpile then, retracing his steps. He faced the birds as he went, not because he feared them, but because he didn't want to stop seeing them.

This is a beautiful place, he said. He looked around the clearing. The birds stood still around him, and around them all were the trees. And you have a lovely flock, too, he said. He bowed slightly, without thinking. He wasn't sure they were a flock, but he didn't know what to call them instead.

The man picked up his wood and then walked into the jungle. He tried to follow the way the peacock had led him, looking for footprints or a few familiar sights. Behind him, he heard the birds again, their calls and their moving about.

When he returned to his camp, he set about building the day's fire. It was dusk already, getting late, and the man had found less wood than he would have liked. Plenty of kindling, but few decent-sized logs. He would consider himself lucky if his fire lasted until midnight.

As the wood burned, the man boiled water for rice. Not much rice left, he thought. Maybe two pounds total in all his stores. He chopped a parsnip into small pieces to add to the rice when it was nearly cooked. The parsnips grew wild, and he had found two the day before the day before.

WHEN HE WAS FOURTEEN, the boy left the cannery and his father and the town where he was from. He didn't run away. He just told his father he was going one morning while they sat at the table eating their oats.

What are you going to do for money? his father asked.

I've saved up some, the boy said.

How much have you saved up? his father asked.

Some, the boy told him.

Well, hey, his father said, don't let me keep you.

His son gathered up his things and went to the door. When he pictured leaving, and he had been picturing it for ten months at least, he imagined a different sort of good-bye. He thought his father might be angry or maybe tearful, but instead he simply walked to the door and opened it. Fare thee well, he said.

The boy went down the stairs and through the cannery works. This, he thought, is the last time I'll walk by here. Everything he did felt imbued, significant. He took a pry bar off a table, thinking he might could use it where he was going, wherever that was. The pry bar was heavy in his hands, cast iron. As he exited onto the street, his father opened a window above and leaned out. The boy thought, Here we go.

His father said, You want to make a bet you're back here by supper?

The boy looked at his father.

How much you want to bet? his father said. He looked up and down the street and he frowned. How much you even got to bet, you piece of shit?

That night, the boy slept outdoors in the middle of a field covered in tall grass. Wind blew through the grass, bending it and making it rustle. The boy liked the sound, the softness of it. He gripped his pry bar in one hand and held it against his chest. Then he relaxed and let his eyes close and he thought, I will be all right.

The next day, the boy wandered with no real aim except to head generally away from the town. He tried to use his pry bar to strike at a squirrel as it was climbing a tree, but the animal was too quick. The pry bar hit the tree trunk and bounced off, back at the boy. His body shook and vibrated, and he dropped the pry bar at his feet. He needed to rest.

Later, the boy came upon an old man collecting wood and asked him if he might help.

The old man said he didn't need any help, especially from some boy.

Then the boy showed him his pry bar, holding it up like the thing spoke for itself.

The old man laughed. What is that? he said. A cudgel?

Pry bar.

Not much call for pry bars, the old man said. He dropped a piece of wood then, by accident, and the boy picked it up.

Give me that, the old man said. He took back his wood and then sought some better arrangement for the load in his arms.

I can carry wood, the boy said.

The old man looked at the boy, considering the offer. I can't pay you, he said.

That's fine, the boy told him. I didn't expect you could.

I might be able to offer you some supper, the old man said, but supper is all. Do you understand me? The old man had wild hair, a beard cut off blunt at the end, and the gently rounded shoulders of someone who once was quite strong.

The boy swore to him that he understood. He would be no trouble.

The old man handed the boy some sticks and then bade him to follow. They walked all day, the old man leading and the boy behind him. The old man moved with a slight limp, though he endeavored to conceal it behind slowness. Over his back, he had slung a sack and some sort of musical instrument, which bounced and shifted about with each step.

That night, the old man built a fire and then fixed supper enough for the both of them. The boy told the old man where he had come from and, while the old man did not ask, also what sort of man his father was. The wood in the fire crackled, and the boy fell silent, listening to the sounds. After a time, when the old man didn't speak, the boy said he was curious to know about his musical instrument.

The old man looked at him funny and then just shrugged. He guessed he didn't have much to say about the thing. He didn't remember where he found it and he didn't know why, really, he kept it with him.

Can I look at it? the boy asked.

I suppose so, the old man said. He fetched it then from among his belongings and, after brushing away some dirt, he handed it over.

The boy took the instrument in both hands and held it so the light of the fire reflected off its surfaces. What is it? he said.

Banjo, the old man said.

Banjo, the boy said. He liked that.

Needs strings, the old man said.

Over the next few days or maybe a week, the old man and the boy gathered wood for fires. The old man taught the boy what he could about what he knew. He taught him the proper names for trees and the five types of fire. He taught him to recognize a parsnip by the look of its leaves. At night, after their fire was burning, the boy told the old man everything he knew: where his grandparents were born and how his parents met and how his mother died while giving birth to him and how his father operated a cannery and what it was like to be inside the cannery, how it sounded when the works were going full blast and how it seemed one's head could not possibly contain all the noise.

The old man posed few questions, but the boy was just happy to go on and on.

At last, when it appeared the boy might be winding down, the old man took up a stick and put one end in the flames. The end glowed and then caught fire. Does it bother you, he said, not knowing any about my life?

The boy shrugged and looked into the fire.

Had the boy not noticed that he had told him almost nothing? The old man wanted to know.

The boy allowed that he had. He just figured the old man would talk in time, when he was ready. And that, moreover, was fine by him.

The old man shoved some small sticks into the heart of the fire. Sometimes, he said, you give someone a thing and the person doesn't give another thing back.

The boy took this in. After a time, he said that, too, would be fine with him. He admired the old man, fiercely so. He wanted to be like him, in a way. It was embarrassing to admit, but nonetheless true. He wanted to live the way the old man lived and do the things the old man did and, in so doing, take his place at the end of some long and unbroken chain, the old man and everyone who came before the old man, going way back, before even the time people had forgotten.

The old man said, I've been alone, on my own, for many years now.

The boy said that didn't bother him any.

The old man looked over the fire, into the dark. Being alone, he said, is what I like.

The boy gathered up some small sticks and gave them to the old man. He was right, the fire did need more sticks. The old man arranged them in his hand and then fed them to the fire. You should go, he said.

In the morning, the old man packed up his things, and the boy did the same. When the old man left, the boy followed a few feet behind. The whole day he trailed him, doing what he did, gathering wood, stopping for lunch, and so forth. At night, the boy built a fire not twenty-some yards from where the old man tended his fire.

For seven days, the boy followed where the old man went. Sometimes he followed close and sometimes he allowed the old man to put distance between them.

On the eighth day, the boy awoke and, as he did every morning, he looked for the old man. Usually he was still asleep, but that day he was gone. The boy hurriedly packed his things and then ran to where the old man had camped. He had left nothing behind. The boy looked around the area, scouring the ground. He had in his mind this notion that the old man would leave him something of value, some token, the banjo maybe, or perhaps just a sign, a telltale mark scratched in the earth, but the boy saw nothing of the sort. He could find no indication of the old man's presence even, save the recently overturned dirt that covered the ashes of his fire.

THE MAN SAW snow flurries in the jungle, sifting through the leaves. At first he thought they were just bits of flowers. They were only falling in one place, in a patch, or else they seemed to be. But then the man held out his hand to catch them. Cold flowers, he thought.

Then he thought: snow. He became quite angry with himself, for his stores were low, and he should already have sought shelter in the caves that pocked the hillside. The air was turning chilly, every day a little bit colder.

The man walked through the jungle, taking all the wood he could carry. Any size, any condition, any type would do. This was no time for discernment. He could sort the stuff later, when he found a cave.

The first cave he came upon had animal scat near the entrance, fox maybe. He rubbed it between his fingers. Fresh, he thought. He searched the cave anyway, looking for anything of use, but found only two handfuls of kindling and some small bones with which he could sweeten a stew.

Other caves seemed similarly occupied. Evictions could get messy, and the man, above all, wanted no mess.

It was late in the afternoon when he came across another cave. Dried nettles covered the entrance, so much so that the man must have passed by several times, seeing nothing. The man moved the nettles aside. Behind them, a large stone was wedged partway into the cave's opening. The man tried to roll the stone back, but could not shift its weight. Using his pry bar and a thick loaf of rock as a fulcrum, he got the stone to move—he had felt it move—but it was too heavy, finally, and he let it settle into its place again. Next, he set his shoulder to the stone, but the thing would not budge. He came at it from every angle, even lying on the ground and planting his feet on its underside. He could make no progress. It was while he was on the ground that he noticed the small rocks, probably hundreds of pebbles, stuck under the stone. Once he moved those aside, the stone rolled almost of its own accord.

Inside the cave, the man found neat stacks of wood, row after row, each stack nearly as tall as he did stand. Good wood, too, all of it. The stacks had been built in layers, with all the logs of one layer facing the man, butt out, and then all the logs in the next layer turned away, and so on. It was a good system, and it reminded the man of his old friend, how he always stacked in this manner. Prevents rot, the old man had said. Even if there's dampness. Because you've got continuous airflow through your pile. He could hear the old man saying these things, telling him, too, how his piles wouldn't topple over either. He wondered then if the old man had been here. And was he still, perhaps, close by? The man searched the cave for some other sign. Could the old man be alive yet? He tried to do the math in his head, guessing how old his friend would have been when they met and then guessing how old he himself was now, but it was just too much math, too much math and anyway too much guessing.

Then it occurred to the man that it was he who had stacked the wood. Maybe he had been here the winter before, or the winter before the winter before. He had just stacked the wood the exact way the old man had taught him. He wasn't sure—he couldn't be sure—but the explanation seemed at least plausible. The man felt annoyed with himself. How he had swelled with so much stupid hope. Did he have no sense? Any, at all?

That night, the man stayed in the cave. He rolled the large stone back over the entrance, sealing himself in. In the dark, he took his pry bar, set it under the stone, and then, with a twist, the stone rolled away to the side, and light from the moon poured in. The man did this several more times until he felt sure of his ability to get out come morning. With the entrance closed, he slept soundly, more soundly than he had, he supposed, in months. He even had a dream.

In his dream, the man lived in a world much like his own. He hunted food and ate parsnips and built fires. Everything was just as it was for the man. He even had his pry bar with him. But at the end of the day, after he built his fire, the man saw himself from above. He saw himself on the ground, standing before his fire, the light of it barely illuminating his feet. Flames rose and fell from the logs, and bits of ash floated into the air, lit up orange before they disappeared. It was then that the man noticed the other fires. From above, they didn't appear to be that far from where the man stood. Distances though were difficult to judge with any accuracy. Even so, there had to be dozens of fires, maybe hundreds, clustering here and there, forming patterns. And where there are fires, the man thought, there are people, or there should be. One person per fire at least. The thought surprised him, and he repeated it, checking it over, examining it for weaknesses, a false conclusion perhaps. The man could see none of this from the ground, of course. The ground was rocky in places, treacherous, and the land was too vast. The coastline curved in and looped out, creating deep, intricate inlets. Wild animals stalked the fires, edging into the dimness and then backing away. The man wanted to tell himself all of this, especially about the other fires. He wanted to shout out instructions, warnings, details about where he should go to find another fire and, beside it, another person maybe, what direction was recommended, how best he should proceed. Remember this, the man thought. Remember how the coast runs, and the hills and, beyond them, the mountains. Remember everything. Remember what you see just the way you see it.

In the morning, the man rolled the stone back and sat on the hillside. A light dusting of frost covered the ground. He fished a ball of old rice out of his pocket and patted it with a little sugar, what he felt he could spare. Show me these people, he thought. Show me their fires. The man waited, but nothing changed and nothing was different. His breath fogged the air. The old man, were he here, would have said the day had some bite. He held the rice ball between his fingertips and sucked at it. Nobody came. Not a sound was heard. Not a sound, except for all the usual sounds. The hill was the hill, and the land was the land, and he was just who he was again, still.

PRAYER FOR WHAT THEY SAID
AND WHAT THEY WERE NOT TOLD

THE HUSBAND AND WIFE needed to get their stories straight. They were going to the beach, to stay with friends, and there seemed some chance—some good chance—that the wife was pregnant.

I'm just going to say I was overserved last night, she said. She wanted some reason, a plausible excuse, for why she wouldn't be drinking. They'd driven all this way, and they hadn't seen their friends in months—not since the fall, actually, or maybe it was the summer before even. And they were at the beach, after all. Drinks were going to be in order, were they not? Maybe a glass of wine or two, some cold beers.

We went out to this sushi place near our house, the husband said. I guess she overdid it a bit on the sake. He rolled his eyes, practicing just the right combination of bemusement and low-grade annoyance.

The key, the wife said, is to keep it simple.

Maybe I shouldn't say anything, the husband said.

You can say whatever. If you want. I don't know, the wife said. The sake stuff is funny.

It's not too desperate, you think?

Funny's always good, the wife said. Funny distracts.

Well, the husband said, I might not say anything is all, if that's all right.

Just do whatever feels natural, the wife said.

They were quiet then, and the dull drone of engine and tires filled the car.

We just can't, you know, protest too much, the husband said. Last thing I want to do is make it this huge thing.

A mile passed, maybe more. The land was flattening out, and the trees were growing sparse and more scrubby, as if every feature were being deleted, until all that would remain was the heat and a hazy horizon.

Because maybe it isn't a huge thing, after all, the husband said. He looked at his wife. Right?

I'm pretty sure, she said.

But we don't really know for sure yet, you said.

No, the wife said. I suppose we don't know for sure.

THEY HAD ONLY just found out that morning, if found out was even the right way of phrasing it. The husband had been in the garage, packing the car, when his wife brought him a suitcase and a grocery bag.

I think this is the last of it, she said. The suitcase bulged in all dimensions.

The husband surveyed their belongings. All their mismatched bags leaned into one another, as if for support through some existential crisis that luggage alone can suffer. Packing was, the husband thought, grim, thankless work. Why did they have so many bags? There came a point every time the husband packed when he asked himself that. It was as if their things—all this stuff, this junk—had snuck up on them while they were doing what, he wasn't sure. Still, he enjoyed the puzzle of packing, the challenge of space divided into oddly shaped forms, and he relished those few moments when things fit—the duffel squeezed just so—as if it had all been arranged according to some grand design.

How's it going? his wife said.

He shrugged and wiped his face on his T-shirt. It's going, I guess, he said.

That was when she told him she was definitely late. She had mentioned it before, and they had talked about it some, but it always seemed just a remote possibility, something to be disproven by the passage of a little more time. She had been late before, after all, occasionally. But then she had never come to him like this, with the news. And she had never said, as she now did, that this time it felt different somehow.

Wow, he said. Okay.

They hugged there, in the garage, and he kissed the top of her head.

I don't know what to say, he said. What do I say?

His wife laughed. I guess we'll see, right?

Right.

The husband started in again with the packing.

Honey? his wife said.

He looked up. What's wrong?

That last bag, the grocery one?

He nodded.

That's snacks for the road, she said.

THE HUSBAND AND WIFE pulled into a broad, gently curving circular drive and came to a stop before a house so massive and so obviously and evidently expensive that neither of them believed it was where they would be staying.

This is it? the husband said. He gazed out his window at a set of sweeping stairs—one of two sets, it seemed, the other up ahead and sweeping away to the left of the house. Flanking the steps were a pair of white marble fish that rose up on their tail fins and stood, the husband guessed, seven feet high.

I think so, his wife said. She was looking again at the directions they had printed out, to make sure.

It's like— the husband said. Actually, he wasn't sure what it was like. He got out of the car and stretched. The fish near him had odd-looking eyes in not quite the right place. It wore a determined expression, though, as if it were trying to dart into the sky and swim away.

The wife came around the car to where her husband was standing. This is definitely it, she said.

It's like it could be a hotel, he said. I mean, look at it. They had come, the husband and wife, to a place where everything was like something else, reminiscent of distant locales and other times. Down the street, a modernist mother ship had landed next to a Mexican hacienda. It just happened that way. In summers past, they had driven by houses not unlike these, and they had gawked at them, just awestruck. It didn't matter how many times they had been to the beach or how many houses they had seen. Who lived here? they asked. Who was it who owned these places?

As they began to unpack, their friends opened the front door and came down the stairs to a landing, where the two staircases joined. Their friends waved and the husband and wife waved back.

Welcome to Stairs-to-Sand, the man said.

The husband looked up, shielding his eyes from the sun, and tried his best to smile. What do you call it again? he asked.

Stairs-to-Sand, the man said. You know— He walked his fingers down the banister.

The husband had heard the syllables as one exotic word, all run together, something like Stahrdezan, a name he imagined must possess some great familial significance they could expect to hear about later. But Stairs-to-Sand, that was something else. The husband had encountered such humility before. It was like when owners of yachts referred to their ships as tubs or little dinghies. Mansions were never mansions anymore. Multimillion-dollar estates were farms, while a sprawling place built into the side of a mountain might be called Hearth House, just because it had so many fireplaces.

Stairs-to-Sand boasted two stories balanced atop stilts, all made in the style of the fanciest Victorian wedding cake. The delicate scrollwork around the windows and eaves looked as if it had reproduced in the night, like algae. The house was going on twenty years old, the man said, a near eternity for beachfront architecture. It was built the summer after Hugo wiped clear the coast. The man's grandfather had owned the place then, having bought part of an acre, cheap, off this guy whose family was originally deeded a significant swath of the state. This was back when nobody could fathom coming to the shore except groups of men, friends, getting away for the occasional weekend, fishing, drinking beers, whatnot. They cooked what they caught. It was nice then, or so the grandfather said, and quiet, very quiet. No bars and taffy stores, and no T-shirt shops or golf courses either. You just couldn't mind the mosquitoes or sleeping in a shack. Later, the grandfather constructed a modest home, and that's where he and the man's grandmother retired. The man grew up coming there, as a kid, staying with his grandparents for long, lazy stretches of the summer. Whatever time he wasn't away at camp, building his character, he spent with them, at the beach. But after the hurricane hit, nobody could see the point in re-creating what once was. Everybody was dreaming big, talking about what could be. Even the insurance man declared the place a sorry teardown. And so, when the policy paid out, the family built this spread. The man, for one, had trouble getting accustomed to it. For years, in fact, he stopped visiting, not even coming for Memorial Day get-togethers. Then his grandfather died, and his grandmother followed not long after. The family lost interest in going and started renting the house out to strangers. It was only recently that the man figured maybe they should try and get some use out of the old place after all.

Rich people, the husband thought. And then: But they weren't that bad, the man and the woman, not really. He only just had to keep reminding himself they were all right. And anyway, almost everybody seemed rich compared to the husband, who had a bad habit of measuring himself against others. How he wanted.

The husband carried their luggage inside, and the woman walked off with the wife, pointing to things as they went, at the roof and the ocean and whatever else there was.

Can I help? the man asked.

The husband said he thought he had it under control, pretty much. It's just one carload, he said. Thankfully.

The husband took their bags upstairs, to the room where, he was told, they would be sleeping. He found one of those fold-out luggage rack things in the closet and set it up in a corner of the room. He put his wife's suitcase on top and unzipped it. It would be easier for her, he thought. Less bending down. Or did she not need to worry about that yet? When he was done, the husband went searching for his wife.

She was downstairs, it turned out, on the deck, looking out over the ocean.

There you are, he said.

Hey, she said.

He hugged her from behind and pulled her close, holding his hands over her stomach, framing it. How are you feeling in there? he said.

She guessed she was okay, she said.

Any big changes to report? he asked.

No, no changes.

172

Waves crashed on the beach below. The ocean churned green into gray. The husband always imagined the ocean was angry. It kind of scared him, too, if he stopped to think about it.

The woman came outside. Oh, she said, sorry. As if she had interrupted them at something serious.

They smiled and parted, everybody sheepish.

I've been sent, the woman said, to get your drink order. She was wearing an apron that said on it, The cook is spoken for.

The woman said she was fine, she'd wait until dinner. The man said he'd love a beer.

What sort? the woman said. She held one hand up before her, ready to tick the kinds off on her fingers.

Whatever's cold, the man said. I'm not picky.

When the woman was gone and the door closed behind her, the husband asked, What's the matter?

Nothing, the wife said.

It's okay if I drink, right? the husband said.

I doubt it'll harm the baby much.

The husband rolled his eyes. If there's a baby, he thought. There was no way to say it that wouldn't sound pedantic. You know what I mean, he said.

THE MAN AND THE WOMAN had started dating in law school, when they were 1Ls. It was the summer before classes began, when all the students pursuing an additional degree in international law—the man and the woman and the wife among them—had come to campus early. At the end of their first week, over drinks at the first of many happy hour mixers, the man saw the woman talking to some other guy. He orbited the perimeter of the party, watching them. He watched them for a while, feeling emboldened by the newness of everything—a new school and the new year to come. He was nearly weightless, so free of any reputation or personal history, such as it was, that he might as well have been reborn. That's when the man walked up to the woman and asked, Excuse me, but what kind of car do you drive? His manner, as the woman later recalled, was at once so brusque and panicked that she figured something must be very wrong. Maybe there had been an accident? Or she was being towed? The woman didn't know. She apologized to the other guy, who said he hoped everything was okay and then left her to deal with this apparent crisis. When the man finally explained himself, how he had only wanted to say hello, the woman found him so endearing that she was flattered and even touched by his odd efforts. They had been together ever since. Their love for each other was great, too, and real, all that. Still, they would not be married, not anytime soon at least, because of tax reasons. Their phrase.

The woman stood to inherit a considerable sum. That much was known, or in any case it was a subject for speculation among the students. Apparently, her family supplied exotic feathers to milliners and clothing designers. A part of that fortune, however large it was, and estimates varied wildly, would almost certainly be hers someday. The man was the twenty-third male of his family to bear his name. He would have been some sort of duke, too, had the United States government not forced his ancestors, generations previous, to renounce their claim to the title. Those were the stories told of him, anyway, the bits of knowledge or, perhaps, myth that the husband acquired soon after meeting the man. The information just came to him, by osmosis, it seemed. One day the husband knew nothing of him, and then the next, he knew as much as anybody. The man dropped his bread crumbs carefully, though, and with a certain studied modesty, not unlike how a Harvard grad can find a way to bend any conversation back to the time he was in school, in

Cambridge, quote-unquote. The man was selective, also. He confided in only a few people, but trusted that they, in turn, would tell others what they had learned. There was, he found, no need to fill in the blanks himself.

As for the man's father, he was a retired admiral, well decorated of course. If the man mentioned his dad, and he didn't very often, he called him the Admiral and took a tone in his voice that made Admiral sound every bit like my old man. The husband wasn't sure if the man spoke with disdain or mockery, exactly, or just plain bitterness. Probably it was all three and that's just for starters. Whatever it was, though, it was the one thing that made the husband think, You know, maybe I could like this guy. The man's mother was a serious potter, but had recently branched out into sculpture. The beach house was populated with her work. Tall, storky birds, beaks agape and about to take wing, perched on side tables. A mangy wolf cub prowled the top of a buffet in the living room, and a badger stood by the back door, its front paws raised as it sniffed at the air. The animals were everywhere, and they all seemed slightly aggressive, or maybe just unsettled. Even a turtle, crawling over the dining-room table, looked ready for a scrap.

They went to good schools, the man and the woman, and they received, for their hard work, for all their trouble, good grades. The man went to a special all-boys boarding school where, secluded in the hills of New Hampshire, or maybe it was Vermont, he was educated in the manner of Alexander the Great, learning swordsmanship as well as ancient Greek from a rotating cast of wizened tutors. Good grades led to prestigious internships, which led to other, more prestigious internships. Advisors and mentors introduced them to friends, associates, colleagues and, like that, doors slid open, passageways were illuminated, and high-ceilinged rooms filled with appreciative applause, cheers, and congratulations, all for them, for their goodness. They had arrived, but then everybody always knew they would. Law school only served to finish them, like the last brushstrokes, applied discerningly, sparingly, to two masterpieces.

The wife and, for that matter, her husband were more misfit-y. The wife worked retail, growing up, and later, made elaborate coffee drinks for college students particular about the fat content of their milk and the quantity of their foam. The husband worked in a grocery store, slicing deli meats and cheeses by the pound. He got to know the butcher, one counter over.

The butcher was a funny guy. Once, he warned the husband to watch himself when he got to college. They were sitting at a picnic table in front of the store, taking their afternoon break. Now there are going to be a lot of girls in college, the butcher said, and they're going to just throw their legs open for any man.

The husband felt his face flush. He sipped at his coffee and tried not to laugh. He had this image in his head of himself, trapped, entangled by legs.

You'll see, the butcher said. He looked over the parking lot, as if searching for someone. All the girls want is a wedding ring, he said. He indicated his own ring, turning it around his finger. And then, of course, they want their babies, he said.

The husband nodded. He moved his coffee cup until the curve of its bottom intersected with the edge of a board. There, he thought, perfect tangent.

You have to be on your guard, the butcher told him.

None of this, in the husband's experience, proved true, not even remotely. But still, he liked the butcher and he thought about him from time to time. He supposed even wrong advice could start off with okay intentions.

OVER DINNER, the couples got to speaking about jealousy. Were they themselves the jealous sort? Were they very jealous, did they think? Had they once been much more so? The talking changed, of course, as talk does, with the couples trading one subject for another, only to circle back always to jealousy. It was heated, at times, but good-natured, basically.

Who was more jealous, the husband asked, men or women?

The wife said she would have to go with men on that one, because in her experience at least, she had more often made them feel jealous than the other way around. To illustrate, she asked if she had ever told them about her ex, the drug dealer.

The man and the woman shook their heads.

Well, she said, he was a really sweet, sweet guy, just, you know, as sweet as can be. He wasn't the brightest, necessarily—he couldn't read, for instance—but he was good to her and so, when they went their separate ways, it was without rancor or even one harsh word.

Hold on, the man said, when you say this guy couldn't read—

She means he couldn't read, the husband said. He had heard this story before.

He couldn't read well, the wife said. I read all his books for him, aloud. He could listen fine.

Was it like a learning disability? the woman asked. She sounded concerned, sensitive, like she'd recently heard a story on NPR about a documentary or something that addressed this very topic.

No, the wife said. I think he was just real bad at it. She didn't know what to say. The man and the woman were forever getting hung up on her first premises. Once, while they were still getting to know one another, the wife happened to tell them about the chicken she had kept as a little girl. It didn't matter what else she said, about how it followed her around or how it came in the house at night, there was, for them, just no getting past the fact of this chicken. Was this in some backyard in Georgia? the woman asked. She was picturing dirt roads, a rickety porch, hayseeds in overalls. The woman wasn't acquainted with people who kept chickens, not as children and certainly not as adults. The wife said it was at her grandparents', actually. They lived in a McMansion located on the seventeenth hole of a country club golf course. I called my chicken Rose, she said.

Anyway, the wife said, years later, when they were all in law school, she received a phone call from her ex. She was, at the time, dating a fellow student, this guy who collected old guitars. He had more than a dozen of them, many quite expensive, though the truth was he could only play them serviceably. At parties, he was known to whip out the opening riff to (I Can't Get No) Satisfaction, but that was about the only thing he played that anyone ever recognized. Most of it sounded like one note wandering aimlessly after another. The wife once described it as real plinky-plinky.

Her ex was in trouble. He had used a fair amount when they were seeing each other and, the wife could only assume, had continued to do so when they weren't. The night he called, for it was night, and quite late, as the wife recalled, he told her he had taken something, he wasn't sure what. Whatever it was, it wasn't what he had been told it was, the fuckers. Of course, he refused to go to the hospital. And so, though it was already late, and though the wife wasn't even sure why he would call her of all people, and after all these years, she said, Tell me where you are, darling. And when he told her, she said she would be right over. As soon as I can get there, okay? You hang on, all right?

Her ex said, Okay, okay.

And you call me immediately, she said, if anything happens, if your condition changes. Immediately, okay?

The wife hung up the phone and told the guitarist what she had to do.

Wait, he said. You're going where?

The wife told him again, though she had been clear before.

I don't get you, he said.

What don't you get? The wife narrowed her eyes some. She set her jaw and closed her mouth and just felt herself breathe. It was as if she were shuttering herself against an approaching storm.

Some guy calls you up, the guitarist said. Out of the blue, as far as I can tell. And then, in the next instance, off you go? On this ridiculous errand? It's like— It's like a comic strip, he said.

He's my friend. She spoke quietly, but with full pressure behind each word.

You called him darling, he said. I couldn't help noticing.

Oh, come on, the wife said. I call everyone darling.

Well, then, better go tend to your friend, the guitarist said. Darling.

The wife collected her things. Her keys, purse, and phone.

As she made for the door, the guitarist trailed after her. Have you even thought about the liability involved?

The wife looked at him. This performance of his.

Well, have you? he said. Have you, for two seconds, thought of the liability?

Liability, incidentally, wouldn't really be a concern, the man said. Not in the way I assume he meant.

That's nice, honey, the woman said. Are you going to bill her later? She smiled at the wife, as if to say, What can you do?

It's the Good Samaritan exemption, the man said. Clear-cut case.

So anyway, the woman asked, was he all right, your ex?

After a time, the wife said. He was running a temperature, though, and then he got really cold and shivery. It came in waves,

179

the hot and the cold, like something was washing over him, pulling his body down. The wife held damp cloths to his forehead and wrapped him in blankets. When he felt like he was going to be sick, she took him to the toilet and sat beside him and rubbed his back and his shoulders and told him everything was going to be all right.

She stayed with him through the night and well into the next day. She brought him water and tea. She made him toast and then she brought him crackers and a cup of chicken broth to dunk them in. When he got his appetite back, she went to the store for some food. She prepared him nice meals, and they ate together. He had had nothing in his fridge, the wife said, except a container of grapefruit juice that had gone bitter and frothy, some baking soda, and a jar of peanut butter she couldn't for the life of her twist the top off of.

They stayed awake, the wife and her ex, just talking. I thought that was best, she said. I don't know where I got that from. Television, I guess.

And when he felt a little better, she read to him, from the only book she could find in his house, which for some reason was A Separate Peace.

A Separate Peace, the man said, like he was trying to put a name to a face.

John Knowles, the husband told him.

It's about these two kids in private school, the wife said. In New England. One's super-outgoing and athletic and the other one is, of course, much more the introvert.

Phineas, the husband said, and Gene.

I feel like I went to school with those guys, the man said.

Knowles is insightful like that, the husband said, We had to read it in, I think, sixth grade. It's the best way they've found to teach public school students all about you kids in private schools.

So anyway, the wife said, my ex got better, and I guess that was that.

And the guitarist? the husband said. He was sitting across from her, which never failed to make him feel lost a bit, or just adrift, as if his chair were breaking free of the table.

He survived, the wife said.

I love when you tell stories, the woman said to the wife. Don't you love her stories? She turned to the man and then to the husband, who nodded and smiled. Just all the crazy people there are in them, she said.

THE LAST TIME they had got together, talk turned to the years of their youth, funny stories about the times one didn't have one's shit together. The implication, never stated, was, Well, look at us now. Except, the thing was, the man and the woman had always had their shit pretty much together.

The woman told about this time in college when she and a bunch of her friends threw plates off the roof of the dorm onto the lawn below. This was the stuff we got from the dining hall, she said. And as she spoke, she struggled not to laugh, trying just to contain her amusement.

It all started, the woman said, when they were faced with the chore of having to tidy up the little kitchen on their floor, and someone said, I have half a mind to throw these plates out the window. Someone else said, That would clean the kitchen. And then someone threw the first plate, and they laughed to see it happen, to be there, and then they all joined in. Someone said, You know what? We should totally go up to the roof, and so they did.

What was really funny, though, the woman said, was the plates didn't break. They just hit the ground, and there'd be a thud, and then maybe they'd bounce a couple of times and then roll to a stop, but they'd never break. They were like indestructible plates, she said. Even when the plates hit other plates. Well, once the friends saw that, they started heaving all the stuff off—cups, saucers, bowls, even the silverware.

Anyway, the woman said. She shrugged her shoulders and chuckled. Now I think of who cleaned all that up? And what did they think, you know, the next morning or whenever? The woman looked down at the table. At the time, she said. At the time, I just couldn't stop laughing. The next day, when she awoke, her stomach muscles were sore. That's how much I was laughing, she said. She held her stomach, as if she could still feel what she had felt.

As the husband listened, he remembered the woman who cleaned his dorm. Everyone was always saying how great she was, when she came up in conversation. She was an older black woman. It was hard to tell how old. She wore a copper-colored wig and caked on the makeup. Years later, the husband read something about her in the alumni magazine, about how she was battling throat cancer and there was a fund set up by some former students, to try to help her out, but he didn't do anything. He thought about it. He had wanted to do something, but then it slipped his mind. The next issue of the magazine brought news that she had died. Donations, it said, may be made in her memory.

The husband said none of this. He tended not to say much, in general. Sometimes, though, he did try to speak, but couldn't find a long enough pause in the conversation. There were pauses, of course, but someone else would always jump in before him. Which was fine. He had waited too long. It was his fault. Or else the conversation just moved on, and what he had to say would have seemed like so much backtracking, like he hadn't been paying attention, when he had, he always had. He could spot an opening in a conversation just fine, could even see it approaching, but then it was gone, just like that, behind him, receding like a missed exit on a highway.

As for the man, he told about a time, one summer, when he was home from boarding school. A bunch of his friends had urged him to ask the Admiral if he could borrow one of his cars. Just for the night, the man told him. And I can be back whenever you say. The Admiral wouldn't hear of it, though. He had ideas about the driving age, the man said. He thought it should be eighteen, with no learner's permit option, and then he thought it should be twenty-one. Initially, the Admiral didn't allow the man to ride in cars with anyone his age, ever, because none of them, he said, could be trusted behind the wheel. With some persistence, however, and not a little arguing, the Admiral eventually backed down and let the man ride with one of his more mature friends. But there would be no borrowing any car.

No, the Admiral said. Absolutely not.

The boys waited until he was asleep and then went outside to the garage. The Admiral had three cars for his personal use: a BMW, an old Cadillac convertible painted baby blue with a pristine white interior, and a pickup truck that he used only rarely but, when asked, said was for hauling stuff around. After some debate, which really boiled down to BMW versus Cadillac, the boys settled on the BMW, especially after the man described to them the insane care the Admiral lavished on the Cadillac's pristine white interior, how he'd shampoo and condition the leather and then buff it out using this special cloth he bought directly from the Cadillac people. We didn't get to sit directly on the seats, the man said. The Admiral always made us spread out beach towels first.

The BMW was, in any case, the man's favorite. This was a 1986 735i, he said. He said the model and year like he expected the string of digits meant something special to everyone. He looked at the woman and the husband and the wife in turn, inviting them to form in their minds a picture of this fabulous car.

The car had a red body—virtually all steel, the man said—and a black interior made of a pebbly leather.

The woman suggested just as gently as she could that maybe the man should tell them what he and his friends did with the car.

But I haven't told you the best part, he said. You want to know the best part, right? The man looked at the wife and the husband, who nodded.

Tell us the best part, the woman said. Please.

It's just the instrument panel, the man said. That's all. It lit up this reddish orange color. It was like being in a submarine or a tank or something. The man held his glass in his hands and looked into his drink. He spoke with a soft voice, almost too soft to hear. The husband had to lean toward him, across the table, the better to listen. Initially, when they first met, he thought the man was trying not to be heard. He just had this way of speaking at the exact volume and pitch of whatever ambient noise was in the room, blending his voice with the sounds made by the refrigerator or the air conditioner. He was that hard to hear. Later, the husband got the feeling that the man wanted people to lean in close, to pay him that extra respect of listening so intently. But the wife said he only talked that way because his father was so loud. That's what the man had told her. When he was young, he said, he swore that, whatever else happened, he would not grow up to be another loud man like the Admiral. He just would not.

You know, the man said, most cars at that time had instrument panels that glowed green.

The man and his friends drove. They drove all night. They drove around. They drove to places in the city they had never been or even thought to go. Then, at two or maybe it was three in the morning, they drove into the ghetto. The ghetto is what they all called it then, the man said. They pulled up to a house, this shack really, with bowing boards and a metal roof, cars in the yard. I'm sure you get the picture, he said. What the man did next is he laid on the horn. At first, he only honked a little, a short, quick burst or two of sound, but his friends so egged him on, that he honked the horn for minutes at a time, nonstop honking. None of them could claim I was chicken, the man said. He honked like that until a light in the house came on. Then he gunned it, just stuck it in gear and let the tires cry. They drove down the road, to some other block, and then they did it all over again—the honking, the squealing tires. They did it until they were bored, and then they went downtown, parked the car, and sat by a fountain. They talked then about how they saw the future and themselves in it. Nonsense, basically, the man said.

Later, when they went back for the car, it was gone. The man couldn't believe it. For a while, in fact, he maintained that where they were standing, where they were looking around, wasn't where he had parked. He thought they'd gotten disoriented there somehow, that maybe they had come at the fountain from the opposite side. But then one of his friends pointed out a no parking sign nobody had seen, and the man felt like he was floating a few inches off the ground and his organs were loose, jostling, bumping into one another, working free of his body. He felt sick.

Nobody wanted to call his parents, to have to wake them up and ask for help, and so the man agreed he would call the Admiral. He walked down the street, alone, to a convenience store, and used the pay phone outside. His father, when he answered, sounded startled, the man thought, and weak, as if the Admiral were stuck still inside the logic of some exhausting dream, trying just to convince himself it was only the phone, the phone had rung, and now he was speaking into it.

Mother and I, the Admiral said, will be there as soon as possible. Probably by the top of the hour.

There was a click on the line, and that was it. The man hung up the phone and heard his quarter drop, and then he checked, out of habit, for change. No luck.

The man returned to his friends. He was in for it, he was sure. The Admiral had been very businesslike on the phone. Too businesslike, if anything. The fact that he hadn't sounded angry—didn't even once swear—only meant he was saving it up for later, stewing, letting the anger compound steadily, like interest earned on the principal offense.

His friends, when the man found them, were chasing one another around the fountain. Like children, he thought. Though half an hour before, he knew he would have been among them, running with them, chasing them. He envied their freedom. He sat on the curb and, resting his chin on his knee, watched the early morning traffic. The city was nice this time of night, slower, darker, with only the essential services up and running. The man had the sense that just a few dozen people, working alone, most of them, kept the whole place going, did everything really.

Not long after, his parents pulled up in the Cadillac. The top was down, like they were out for a spin. Hey, Dad, the man said. Mom.

The Admiral faced forward and didn't answer except with the slightest of nods.

Your father, his mom said, would like you to make sure your friends put out the towels. Can you do that, please? She smiled then, like she was trying to say something with her eyes, a secret message for him alone, but the man couldn't imagine what it might be.

He called to his friends and then spread the towels across the backseat. When everyone was inside, he got in the front and sat between his parents.

All right, the Admiral said, what do you say we go retrieve my car? He spoke loudly, like a tour guide. He was just so— The man paused, hunting for the word he wanted. Chipper, he said, at last. He was so unbearably chipper.

The man's friends, of course, all laughed. They ate it up, he said.

Any of you gentlemen been to the impound lot? the Admiral asked.

No one answered. Then one of the man's friends spoke up. No, sir, he said.

Well, the Admiral said, You're in for a real treat, then.

For the rest of the ride, the Admiral persisted with his chatting. He asked the boys about how school had gone that year and how they had fared at their various sports. He wouldn't take any pat answers, either. No all rights or pretty goods and leave it at that. The Admiral wanted to know more. What was such-and-such like as a lacrosse coach? he asked. That sort of thing. The man couldn't believe it. What an act, he thought. And yet, what an accomplished act it was. He fully expected his friends would now doubt everything he had told them about his father. All my horror stories, the man said. He shook his head. What a great guy your dad is, they would say. He could already hear it. And so funny, too. Et cetera. Et cetera. The man did their voices high-pitched and whiny, as if his friends were a pack of elves.

While the Admiral drove and gabbed, the man tried to tune him out, letting his voice merge with the hum of the road. He looked at his father's hands on the steering wheel, gripping it at ten and two, just like he always instructed. His hands looked old to the man. Like old man's hands, he thought. The man had never noticed before, but as they passed into and out of the streetlights, he saw his father's hands flashing in the light, and he thought, Dad is old. His skin was loose, almost transparent, and foxed with dark spots and blotches. His knuckles were like dice, all sharp edges and corners. The man got to wondering about when he was born and how old his father had been. Was it bad, not to know? He occupied himself with math, adding and subtracting years from their lives. Outside, a long and unbroken line of dubious businesses and restaurants unrolled before him, coming into view and then falling away. He saw one place that sold liquor and ceiling fans. In the same store.

The impound lot was surrounded by a tall chain-link fence topped with curlicues of concertina wire. Men with dogs patrolled the rows of cars, and sodium vapor lights mounted high on poles bathed everything in yellow. At the Admiral's insistence, the man's mother remained in the car, with the top up. You want to listen to the radio? the Admiral asked her. He was leaning into the car. She shrugged. Okay, he said. Well, I'll leave you with the keys. Just, whatever you do— The Admiral straightened up and tucked in his shirt. Just don't leave us here. The man's friends laughed. This was turning out to be an excellent evening for them.

Come on, boys, the Admiral said. And they headed toward a mauve trailer at the corner of the lot.

Inside, a clerk sat at a counter, hiding behind an ancient computer terminal. She stared vacantly into a monitor, the fingers of her hands poised over her keyboard. Can I help you? she asked. She didn't look up from the monitor, just spoke, evenly, like a recording.

I believe you have my car, the Admiral said.

License registration, the clerk said. She pronounced it as one word, as if it were just the one thing she needed.

The Admiral produced his documents. He was the sort of person who not only had his papers in order but knew, in advance, which forms of identification he would need. At home, he kept the originals filed away in his desk or stored in the safe. He had a whole system, the man said. For a while, he was making copies of everything, too, and getting them notarized, just to maintain a hedge against any future inconveniences.

The boys here were driving, the Admiral said. He leaned on the counter, friendly-like, as if he had just stopped by for a visit.

Don't need the blow-by-blow, the clerk said. Just license registration.

The Admiral rapped his knuckles a couple of times on the counter and made a funny face for the benefit of the man's friends.

Can you tell me how long this will take? he asked the clerk. He wasn't being rude. The man, of all people, knew how rude his father could be. Still, the Admiral was getting a little short.

The clerk looked up from her monitor. Honey, she said, the more you keep on talking, the longer it's going to take.

Just looking for an estimate, the Admiral said. That's all.

I got to key in all your information first, the clerk said.

How about you just ballpark it for me? the Admiral said.

The clerk looked up at the ceiling and thought for a few seconds. From the blank expression on her face, it seemed she had left, gone somewhere to locate an answer. Probably an hour, she said, with all the paperwork.

An hour? the Admiral asked. He glanced at his watch and then looked back at the clerk, trying to reconcile the one to the other. You jokers haven't even had the car for an hour, he said.

You'd think, the man said, she had told him it would be a year, give or take.

If you're in a hurry, the clerk said, and you seem like you are, you can pay the expedited rate.

Expedited rate, the Admiral said

The clerk nodded. Expedited rate is for expedited service, she explained.

The Admiral was beside himself. Is that allowed? he asked. In this country?

The clerk shrugged. Information's on the wall over there, she said. She indicated a piece of paper, lime green and taped at its four corners.

In the end, the Admiral decided against the expedited rate. He had taken to referring to it, loudly, as expedited rape, until the man asked him, Please, stop with the rape stuff, okay?

The expedited rate cost more than double and yet it offered, the Admiral said, as far as he could see, no explicit guarantee of faster service. He just wouldn't let it go, the man said. The Admiral was the type of man who could gnaw on some trivial insult for days, weeks, before he realized he had been chewing on his own leg. When he was done laying his whole rationale out for the clerk, as if she cared, the Admiral folded his arms over his chest and glared across the counter. How much faster would expedited even be? he said. Assuming I wanted it, which I don't.

The clerk couldn't rightly say. Maybe a little faster, she said. She still needed to key in all the same information, regardless.

Well, that's wrong, the Admiral said. It's just wrong.

Sir, the clerk said, I don't make the rules around here.

The Admiral took a seat, and the man sat beside him. The others rested on the floor or leaned against unoccupied stretches of wall. The trailer was packed, but people were cow-eyed and, mostly, subdued, just resigned to their fate, however long that would take to be made manifest. Some lacked the proper license registration. Or a part of their license registration was, they said they were pretty sure, locked in the car, probably in the glove compartment. Every so often, a guy who worked in the lot entered the trailer, called out some number, and then escorted the lucky individual outside, to the impounded vehicle, to fetch whatever it was the clerk still needed. The guy moved slowly, listing from side to side as he walked. He would only ever take one person at a time. Rules were rules.

A few people were waiting for friends to show up with the money. Two men spoke German. They sliced and chopped the air with their hands, gestures that couldn't have been anything other than a long preface to a longer fistfight. A woman held a baby to her shoulder while she tried also to mind a child who, every few minutes, announced that he wanted to go home now, and then, a few minutes later, announced that he wanted to play video games now. A man in a wheelchair was parked near the door, snoring in his sleep. Everyone was tired. They slouched in their seats. For entertainment, or maybe just for a brief respite from boredom, they stared at one another. The man stared, too. When he caught anyone staring at him, the person looked away, at someone else. It was the one unwritten rule of waiting. A television bolted high up in one of the corners was tuned to a network that blared health tips aimed at seniors and those suffering from diabetes.

For the next hour—and the process did take almost exactly an hour—the Admiral lectured the boys about how what was going on at this impound lot was nothing less than institutionalized bribery. That's what this expedited rate is, the Admiral told them. Just a bribe by a misleading name. He looked at the lime green sign and then looked away, newly disgusted to find it still there.

You just realize, the Admiral said, at times like this, how tenuous civilization is and how little separates us, really, from thieving kleptocracies or outright barbarism.

One of the man's friends started to raise his hand, like in a class. Would you say it was a slippery slope–type situation? he asked.

191

The man wondered if some fun was being had at his father's expense. He wasn't altogether sure. There was just something in the tone, he said, an overripened earnestness perhaps, as if the words themselves were winking. The man felt pained, pierced and then torn in several directions at once. He was embarrassed, of course, but he was also defensive, even protective, of his father. The Admiral was, he knew, ridiculous at some level, but it was the ridiculousness he had breathed his whole life. If it made him cough at times, it had also somehow sustained him.

The Admiral, in any case, was unfazed. He knew well enough how to handle insubordinate elements. I wouldn't call it a slippery slope, he said. He pronounced the words with distaste, as if forced to eat something foul. It's more like a piece of a fabric or a tapestry. Do you understand me?

The man's friend said he did, he did understand.

Now the danger arises, the Admiral said, when the fabric starts to come unraveled. And let's say nobody notices, because life appears pretty much as it was. Maybe it's a little shittier around the edges, excuse my French. Maybe you got some offers for expedited service where before there was just one single standard for all mankind. He stared at the clerk, who was back to communing with her monitor. And maybe you have an uptick in the population of fee rats and other vermin, people just happy to collect the money and ask no questions and say I didn't make any sign, but over time, I'm telling you, it all adds up, and the fabric weakens and, before you know it, you're wearing animal pelts and stockpiling rocks, and you're checking out your neighbors to see which one of you lazy numbnuts am I going to eat first?

The Admiral scanned the room. What a peculiar collection of humanity. What a sad parade of the flesh. The guy in the wheelchair was at the counter, checking on the disposition of his case.

The Germans had made up and were speaking nostalgically about something on the television. A segment was on in which a roomful of old people were doing aerobic exercises while sitting in chairs pretty much identical to the ones in the trailer. It was like looking through a window into the future, the man said.

He and his friends were quiet, or maybe just tired.

I'm joking, of course, the Admiral said. Well, not about the fabric and the fee rats and all that. Just the part about the eating.

The man asked the Admiral if they could talk, outside maybe.

Dawn was approaching. Pink light at the edges of their world. The Admiral waved to his wife and then mimed how she should just stay in the car for the time being. Everything was fine.

She mimed back what was going on, and why was this taking so long?

The Admiral shrugged and looked up at the sky. What could he do?

The man said he just wanted to apologize is all.

Okay, the Admiral said.

I know what I did was wrong, the man said. And I know you and Mom are disappointed with me, and that I'll have to be punished still—I know I will have to be punished—but I just wanted to say how sorry I am.

You don't think coming here is punishment enough? the Admiral said.

The man laughed. I don't know, he said. Maybe.

Two men inside the impound lot approached the gates and slid them open. One car emerged, and then the gates closed behind it. The car sped away, free.

This place, the Admiral said, it's depressing. It's survival of the most patient in there. He shook his head. Not that patience is a bad thing, ordinarily, but come on.

Cable television might be nice, the man said.

193

The Admiral nodded. Couldn't hurt, he said.

They sat down on the concrete steps that led up to the trailer and watched everything turn a bit lighter.

Once, sitting outside like this, the Admiral had taught the man how to make a fist. It was years before, the man said. He was six, maybe seven. He was guessing, he said. The man had spent the better part of the morning and afternoon helping the Admiral replace the disc brakes on the Cadillac. He fetched him wrenches, whatever he asked for. The Admiral did his own automotive work, and he was proud of that fact.

When they finished with the brakes, the Admiral pulled a couple of lawn chairs out of the garage, and they sat. It was quiet out, just the two of them. The Admiral said, Let me see you make a fist.

The man made his fist. He tucked his thumb under his fingers and squeezed his hand tight, until his knuckles turned pale. The man showed the woman and the husband and wife what he meant. He looked at his hand. I haven't thought about this in years, he said.

The Admiral tapped the man's thumb. Don't do that, he said. You hit someone like that, you'll snap your thumb in two. Do like this, he said. The Admiral brought his fingers into his palm then and lay his thumb across them, as if he were sealing them in place. That's a good fist, he said.

The man tried it. It seemed wrong somehow, the thumb on the outside.

You just have to practice, the Admiral said. You have to do it until it comes natural.

For days and weeks after, at unexpected times, the Admiral asked the man to let him see that fist, and every time the man showed him the right fist.

A tow truck pulled up and honked its horn, and the men came from inside to open the gates.

You know what would be really funny? the Admiral said.

The man had no idea.

If we just drove off. The Admiral made his hand into a car and cruised it down an imaginary road. Just leave your friends on Dr. Moreau's island here and take your mother out for pancakes.

The man liked the idea. He really did. The meanness of it made him laugh, thrilled him even, if he was being honest. Pancakes, he thought. And Mom and Dad and me.

The Admiral was quiet. I hope I didn't embarrass you too much, he said. With your friends.

No, the man said. Everything's all right.

THE HUSBAND AND WIFE had a small room with two twin beds and a window that faced the street. Part of going on vacation meant enduring crap beds and less-than-ideal sleeping arrangements. At least for the husband and wife it did. Another summer they had gone to the beach with a friend's family and crashed on a pullout sofa in the middle of the living room. A raised metal bar ran between them. In the morning, when the family awoke, the husband, clad in improvised pajamas of some sort, excused himself to put on regular clothes. Sorry, he said, for my appearance. Every morning, the same story. But this was what they could afford right now. That's what they told themselves.

All the guest rooms at Stairs-to-Sand were identical, it seemed, like cells, with the same furniture positioned the same way. They even had the same art hanging on the walls. Bright patchwork fish by the door and, above the dresser, a lonely lighthouse overlooking an empty beach.

The woman explained the accommodations, as if obligated. The twins made the house more desirable, she said. As a rental.

She looked around the bedroom and frowned slightly. I'm not sure when we'll redecorate, she said. But I guess the house does sleep more this way.

The husband and wife nodded, like they could relate.

The master's nice, the woman said. Do you want to see it?

The husband looked at his wife. If he could plead with his eyes, he did.

Tomorrow, she said. I'm just so tired. The drive and all, you know.

The woman nodded. Yeah, she said. Well, can I get you guys anything? Towels or whatever?

They shook their heads and thanked her again, telling her how much they appreciated being able to come to the beach and how nice it was that they could stay with them, and then, at last, they were alone. They lay on their beds, the husband on his, the wife on hers, and they looked at the ceiling. The husband reached his arm out to his wife. They could hold hands if they both stretched.

How are you feeling? he said.

Okay, she said. Glad to be here, I guess.

Any pregnancy stuff going on? he asked.

She shrugged. You don't have to keep asking me, you know.

I want to, he said.

Well, she said, I feel light-headed a little, maybe.

Could just be the sun, the husband said. He looked over at her. Not that you couldn't also be pregnant. I just mean, he said, that I get light-headed sometimes from the sun. All that heat.

It's okay, she said.

The wife got out of bed. I guess I'll get ready, she said. I really am tired. The husband propped himself up on an elbow and watched her undress. There could be no end to her taking her clothes off, to being naked, as far as he was concerned.

When she was done in the bathroom, the husband brushed his teeth and whatnot and then he lay down beside his wife and held her.

Do you have enough room? she said.

He was fine. Can we stay like this? he said. Just for a little while, until you're sleepy?

Sure, the wife said. As long as you don't fall off.

The husband found a comfortable spot and breathed in the air around her hair. I feel like we've been apart the whole day, he said.

That's silly, his wife said. We've been together the whole time.

Well, but we were always apart, though, he said. Like in the car, you were way over on the driver's side, and I was way over on the passenger's side.

The wife made a sound like she thought he was being absurd.

Or at dinner, he said, there you were, clear across the table.

You'd stay in bed all day if you could, the wife said.

In the dark, the husband smiled. The thought does hold great appeal, he said.

For a second, they were quiet. They listened to the sounds the house made and they heard each other breathe.

I was thinking some about your ex, the husband said.

The wife made another sound.

Yeah, the husband said. And I guess, I don't know, I was wondering, have I ever told you about the time I took some LSD this guy had?

What guy? the wife said.

Well, it was before I met you, he said. It was on my birthday.

The husband was living then with his parents and back to working at the deli counter. He had dropped out of college, but only for the year. He just needed a little break from things. So anyway, he was alone, had nothing to do, but he had this stuff from a guy at the deli. The guy was born with one normal arm and one arm that never developed. It looked about the size of a baby's arm but more shriveled, the husband said. The other thing about this guy was that he had been in a band that went on to achieve brief national renown, though he had quit the group a few years before they became famous. He played guitar, the husband said. You wouldn't think he could, and it looked strange to see, his one shriveled arm working up and down the fret board, but he was really good.

Anyway, the husband said, this guy had sold him the stuff one day. He didn't normally sell. He just needed some money, quick. At the time, the husband wasn't sure he even wanted it. He bought it just to be nice, really.

At first, the husband said, nothing happened. He was down in the basement, which was where he slept, though it also doubled as the laundry. He didn't know if it was bad stuff, or if that was just the way it worked, slowly. He told his parents he was going for a walk.

His father asked, Have any plans for your birthday, big guy?

Not really, the husband said.

He walked down the hill to the corner and then he walked into town. It wasn't far, but he was sweating through his clothes. I thought maybe I should sit down, the husband said. That the drug was starting to take effect or whatever. He found a bus shelter and lay across the bench, one arm over his forehead and the other dangling to the ground. After a time, a bus appeared. The door opened, and the husband heard the driver ask him something. He sat up. What? he said.

The driver said whatever he had said again, and the husband just told him he was fine. Then he waved his hand at him. The driver scowled and looked away, out his side mirror.

The husband tried to think if he had offended the driver, but came up empty. In any case, there was no fixing it, assuming anything needed fixing, because people were getting off the bus. The husband watched from behind the bus shelter. Seemed safer there, he said. With the plexiglass. That was when he had the sense that the people were part of the bus, and the bus was ridding itself of them, because they were parts it had no use for anymore, just the junk. The weird thing was, the husband said, they didn't look any different. They looked just like people getting off a bus. Like how you'd expect.

The husband went home and stayed in the basement. For the next thirty-some hours, he didn't sleep.

In the morning, or what he figured must be the morning, he told his mother he was not well.

Do you need anything? she asked. She was standing at the top of the stairs.

No, he said. I'll be fine. I just need to rest.

Well, I'm coming down, she said. I need to check on you myself.

Mom, he said, no. Don't come down here. Please.

She stopped on the steps. He listened.

Whatever it is I got, he said, I'd hate for you to get it.

His mother retreated up the stairs. He heard her on the landing, the door creaking on the hinges as she opened it. The familiar sounds of his life.

Mom, he said.

Yes.

Could you call into work for me? he said. If it's no trouble?

Sure, she said. I can do that.

Minutes later, though the husband said it seemed like another day, or else a dream, his mother was on the stairs again. She said his manager was on the line, that he wanted to speak with him, but the husband just said he was too sick to talk. He was still sweating, like he had after his walk, except he hadn't done anything. He hadn't moved, hardly. He did go upstairs to the kitchen, once, to get some crackers or something, but that was it. He had waited until his parents were in another part of the house, because he didn't want to see them. He didn't want to see anyone. When he heard them coming, he crept back down the stairs. His heart raced, and his body shook, and he couldn't keep food down. He told himself, One more day of this, and I'll get help. I will.

It was pretty scary, the husband said. He nudged his wife. When she didn't respond, he shifted his weight on the mattress. Springs squeaked. Was she sleeping? Her breathing was slow, quiet.

Then, at last, she spoke. Sounds bad, she said.

I was scared, he said.

For a while, the wife didn't say anything, and the husband thought, once more, that perhaps she was asleep.

Why are you telling me all this? she said.

I don't know, the husband said. Except he did. He hadn't worked it all out in his head, but what it came down to was that he wanted her to care for him, just as she had cared for her sweet, addicted old boyfriend. It was impossible, of course, what he wanted, but he wanted it still. If anything, the impossibility only made him want it more. He just wanted to be taken care of. Nursed, that was the word. He wanted to receive such love from her. And love is what he called it.

I just thought, the husband said, it was selfish, what that guy did, your ex.

How do you mean? his wife said. She turned over to face him.

Calling you up and all. Out of the blue, as I think you put it. It's like the definition of selfish.

He needed help, the wife said.

I know, the husband said. I know. And, it's great that you helped him. It's great that you could. But I'm just asking, Did he need that help?

The wife pulled the covers up over her shoulder, so that all the husband could see was her face.

Because maybe he wanted help, the husband said. I can see that. And maybe he wanted you, specifically, to help. That, too, I can see.

I don't think, the wife said, he was in any condition to be hatching schemes.

Okay, the husband said. Maybe not. Maybe I'm wrong. It just made me remember the time I took that stuff. That's all.

Well, you're clearly the better person, the wife said. Never calling anyone. Never asking for help. Is that what you want me to say?

No, the husband said. I don't know.

LATER, the husband got out of bed. This is really uncomfortable, he said. His wife didn't make a sound. I think my arm's gone numb, he said. He got into his bed and pulled the covers up. He looked at his wife, at the outline of her shoulder and her hair, and he whispered good night.

He couldn't sleep, however. The husband tried lying on his back and then he tried lying on his side. He tried facing his wife and then he turned away from her and tried that. His wife could sleep anywhere, at any time, even after a big fight, it didn't matter. He thought back over what he had said and what she had said. He wasn't sure, finally, if they were fighting or not. He guessed they had been, sort of. It was heading in that direction, at least.

The husband sat up in bed and looked around the room at their belongings. All their stuff, everything they had brought, it was here. The dark forms of suitcases open on the floor. Piles of clothes beside them. It looked like they were running from someone, like they had just grabbed what they could and fled. He had tossed the shirt and pants he had worn that day onto the floor. They were at the foot of his bed, or near it, balled up. He looked for them in the dark, feeling around on the carpet. When he found his clothes, he dressed quickly, as though he needed to be somewhere, and then he went downstairs.

The man was sprawled out on the sofa, watching television. The lights in the room were off, and his face glowed blue-white, like the moon. He saw the husband and raised the clicker to his forehead in a salute. Greetings, he said.

Can't sleep, the husband said.

Me neither, the man said. I always think it's too damn quiet here. Not enough helicopters and sirens. Then I get used to it, though, and I don't want to leave.

The man got wrapped up again in whatever he had been watching. His jaw went slack, and his expression froze, and then only his eyes moved. The husband glanced at the TV. It looked like old music videos, maybe a countdown, he couldn't tell. He might almost feel nostalgic, if he tried. After a while, a commercial came on, and the man muted the sound.

Can I get you anything? he asked. Beer, wine?

The husband said he was fine. He was still standing, half in the room, half thinking he should leave, go for a walk or a drive, just do something. He sat instead. He propped his feet on the coffee table and stared at the television.

The man skimmed through half a dozen channels before finding a movie that hadn't been going for very long. You seen this? he said.

The husband wasn't sure. It looked familiar, vaguely. He may have watched part of it, or maybe he'd read about it online. I'm not sure, he said.

It's your average teen horror type of thing, the man said. You know, world's going to shit of some variety, parents are nowhere, police are incompetent, maybe even corrupt, and so the kids have to band together and do the job themselves.

On the television, a woman ran to a house and tried the door. It was locked, and the house was dark. The character screamed and pounded on the door. Behind her, automatic sprinklers were on, watering the front lawn.

I'm afraid sister's not long for this shitty world, the man said.

Could be a false alarm, the husband said. The unbearable tension before a bit of relief.

Too early for relief, the man said. Sister's the sacrifice. She dies and then everyone else wakes up and says, What the hell's happening here, in our quaint little village where nothing bad ever happens?

You're probably right, the husband said.

Not long after, the character died, her neck snapped. Her body lay in the grass. Her eyes were open and unfocused, empty.

She does a good dead, the man said. I'll give her that.

The sprinklers shot long arcs of water into the air and made a sound like tsk, tsk, tsk. And then, like that, it was the next morning. There was sun and there were birds, and there was a body to be found.

I wonder how long she had to stay like that, the husband said.

The man shrugged. The only real question with these movies, he said, is will there be breasts in them, and if so, how many and for how long?

They watched the movie for a while then, more captivated than entertained. People died in ingenious ways: on an elliptical machine and at the mercy of a juicer. One got boiled in a hot tub. Another was run through with a car antenna. It was as if death were the ultimate stunt, the thrill toward which they all hurtled.

When the movie got too predictable, the man muted the sound and asked the husband if his wife had told him much about Hong Kong.

The husband said, Yeah, some, I guess.

He had heard all the stories, most of them, he figured, several times. The gist of it was that the man, the wife, and a sizable contingent of law students had descended on Hong Kong one summer, ostensibly to take classes. They traveled around, too. Thailand, Laos. Mainland China. A few flew off to New Zealand one weekend on a spur-of-the-moment type of thing. A bunch of them had signed up for the program. Except for the woman. The woman divided her time, as she put it, between New York, where her mother lived, and Caracas, where she worked with her father and uncle, doing deals for the feather company. As for the man, once he was over in Hong Kong, he slept around quite a bit. Everyone knew he was doing it. That's what the wife had said anyway. There was something, too, about a couple of students from Russia, or maybe it was the Ukraine. The husband couldn't recall the details, save that the man had, basically, hooked up with them. Hooked up being the wife's term. The husband didn't like hooked up much, all its studied vagueness disguised as innocence.

She ever tell you about the rat? the man asked.

The husband shook his head.

The man smiled. I thought not, he said.

What rat? the husband said. What are you talking about?

Well, you know we were staying in these old dorms, the man said. And in many ways, it was like being back in college. And people acted the part, right? They drank all the time, partied until all hours, and then they dragged themselves to dim sum in the afternoon.

I don't remember a lot of dim sum in college, the husband said. Maybe that's just me, though.

Anyway, the man said, we had our own rooms, which were small and unpleasant. Imagine a coffin, he said, except with a porthole on one end that looked onto the roof of some other building.

On their last night in Hong Kong, the wife and the man stayed up late, talking in the common area. All the rooms opened onto one of these common areas, the man said. It was the one decent place to sit. There they talked about their plans, such as they were, what they wanted to do with their lives and what they would sooner die than have to do, so help them.

It was while they were talking that the rat ran out from under the chair where the wife was sitting. It was a big thing, the man said. I've seen smaller cats in my time. And it had these weird red eyes, too. The rat stopped in the middle of the room, looked around, and then ran back where it had come from, straight toward the wife.

Well, the man said, she screamed, of course, and she jumped up onto her chair, and I jumped onto mine, and we stood like that for a while, looking around, asking each other, Did we see it? Did we see that goddamn rat?

What the fuck, the wife said. She hopped from one chair to another until she was standing with the man in his chair. Then she looked back at her chair, trying to see underneath. Where is that thing? she said.

They sat down again, and they tried to talk, but it was hard not to think of the rat. At last, the man said he had to get some sleep.

You're just going to leave me to the rat? the wife said.

My flight is ass early, the man said.

The wife scanned the carpet. She hadn't touched her feet to the floor in minutes, not since the rat. She was wondering if there might be a way, in fact, to avoid doing so for the remainder of her stay. I don't think I can sleep, she said.

You should try, the man said.

The wife shook her head. I'll close my eyes, she said, and just think of that rat. I know I will.

Still, the man said.

Its eyes were red, the wife said.

The man nodded.

I thought maybe I imagined it.

No, the man said.

Red eyes, the wife said.

They said their good nights then and turned in.

Later, the man was lying in bed when he heard a soft knock at his door. It was the wife. She had wrapped herself in her blanket. Can I stay with you? she said. I just can't be in my room alone.

The man said he guessed so.

Thank you, the wife said. I wasn't sure you'd be awake.

I think I was sleeping, the man said. Or I almost was.

Well, thank you. The wife spread her blanket over his bed and crawled underneath.

The man stood beside the bed. How should I sleep? he said.

However, the wife said. She lay facing the wall, already sounding tired.

The man got into bed and lay on top of the covers. It seemed the right thing to do, he said. You know?

The husband nodded. Sure, he said. While the man talked, the husband had alternated between keeping tabs on the movie and looking at a vase of flowers on the coffee table between them. They were lilies, the husband thought, though he wasn't sure. He was always mixing up his flowers, confusing lilies with irises, as stupid as that sounds. In any case, the flowers were in full, roaring bloom, the petals spread so wide, they were bent back on themselves, and the stamens—or were they the pistils?—the husband couldn't remember—were pushed forward. The whole bouquet was aching, the husband thought, to get pollinated.

Anyway, the man said, I woke up early. It was still dark outside. I packed my things and then I told your wife I was going.

She got out of bed and wrapped her blanket around her. Okay, she said. Bye.

I remember, the man said, she sounded so sleepy.

They walked into the common area, and the man made some joke about it being too early even for rats, and the wife shook her head.

Not funny, she said.

The man called the elevator, and then they waited, watching the line of numbers light up above the door, as if the machine required their complete concentration to operate.

When the elevator arrived, the man got on and waved to the wife, and the wife, from inside her blanket, waved back.

Get some sleep, the man said. You look awful.

As the elevator door closed, the man watched the wife turn toward her room. Bye, he said.

Is that it? the husband asked.

Yeah, the man said. Basically.

Why basically?

Because basically, the man said, that's it.

So nothing happened, the husband said. He wasn't sure why he cared, or if he cared. There was the secrecy of it, he supposed, maybe. How had he never heard any of this before? But then, they hadn't even met, he and his wife.

No, the man said, nothing happened. He threw up his hands and scratched angry quote marks in the air. Nothing, he said.

The man sat up and looked at the television. The clicker was in his hand, and he was playing with the buttons, pressing at them, but not enough to change the channel or anything. I think about that time, the man said. Sometimes. Maybe I think about it a lot, actually. He looked at the husband. I don't want to make you mad, he said.

The husband nodded, not really looking at him, though. There was a place where the table met the vase. That's where he was looking. There was a flower petal on the table, and scattered around it was bright orange dust, pollen.

I ask myself, the man said, What would have happened if, right? What if I had been more forward or done something or even just said something? Maybe my life would have gone differently. Is that ridiculous? the man asked. To say?

Maybe nothing would have happened, the husband said.

Sure, the man said. Absolutely. Maybe nothing would have happened. But I still wonder. I can't help it. It's like the memory of it—my memory—is closed up in some room, stored away, and I'm crawling up to the door. I'm always crawling, always on my hands and my knees, and I sniff at the door, and I scratch at it. I want inside that room.

The husband was trying to look at the matter in as broad a light as possible. That's how he thought of it, as a matter, a complex shape to rotate in his mind. He wanted to consider it from various angles, as if he were viewing a finely cracked urn in some museum. The husband was just trying to be generous. The man was talking about his wife, yes, but if he weren't, if he were just talking about someone else, some fleeting encounter years before, a hook-up in a Hong Kong dormitory, the husband imagined he'd feel sorry for the man. What a sad guy, he'd think. That's what the husband was trying to bear in mind, anyhow. The man was like an athlete remembering a bad pass, the ball tipped right into the other team's hands, another ancient moment of split-second personal humiliation to view over and over: himself, bent at the waist, resting his hands on his knees, the rain of flashbulbs around him. Except in the man's case, there wasn't anything but the rat. That, the husband decided, was what made him so sad. He had nothing worth remembering.

The husband said, I had a girlfriend once who had a pet rat.

A rat, the man said, like he was weighing the pros and cons. I'm afraid that would have been a deal breaker for me.

It wasn't a big rat, not like yours, the husband said. It was probably like— He held out his hands and looked from one to the other, adjusting them until they were spread about six inches apart or so.

That's with the tail or without? the man said.

With.

That's still plenty large, the man said, for a rat.

She loved that thing, the husband said. It crawled across her shoulders. It went up and down her shirt. And it liked to nestle at the back of her neck. Right here, he said. The husband got up and touched the place on the man's neck where the rat liked to go. It used to hide in her hair, he said. He sat back down. If we were talking, the husband said, sometimes I'd see the rat poke its little nose around her neck, smelling the air or whatever rats do.

That's too creepy, the man said.

Or sometimes I'd reach to touch her neck, the husband said, to kiss her, you know, and there the rat would be.

Jesus, the man said. Are you sure this girl wasn't a witch?

She wanted to be a forest ranger, the husband said.

The man nodded, thinking. He didn't know any forest rangers.

Toward the end, the husband said, when we were still dating but only because we hadn't, one of us, figured out how to say maybe we shouldn't be dating anymore, I looked at the rat as my rival.

The man laughed a little.

You know, the husband said, we still did stuff, she and I, and we still talked, but only for a little while, because the talk petered out and then nobody said much for a long time. It wasn't a comfortable silence, either. I tried to think of something to say, because I knew I should say something, but all I could think was maybe we had run out of things to say, like that was it. That's when I got to thinking, The rat is closer to her than I am.

Got more action anyway, the man said.

Yeah, okay, but not just action, the husband said. Actual close-ness, that's what I'm talking about. She was closer to the rat than to me. The husband said it slowly, like he was putting the pieces together for the first time. I would think about that, he said.

What happened to her? the man said.

I'm not sure, the husband said. We lost touch, I guess.

She become a ranger?

Actually, the husband said, she did.

I like that, the man said. The thought made him just beam. Do you think about her much?

Not really, no, the husband said.

Something bright flashed on the television, an explosion. They both watched as a fire consumed meadows, fields, and houses. Horses pulled carriages through the flames. There was smoke and ash and people stumbled about, lost, forsaken. Through it all, one man stalked another with a stick.

I'm thinking this is another movie, the man said. Either that or someone's having a really bad dream.

The husband watched for a while and then he looked away, out the window. It had to be late. I should probably call it a night, he said.

Yeah, the man said. Me too.

But nobody moved. After a bit, the husband said he did actually think of his old girlfriend. Not often, he said, but, you know, from time to time. Except, it's strange, he added. Because I think of her the way I might think about a country I once traveled to. Do you know what I mean?

The man didn't. Sorry, he said.

The husband leaned back and looked at the ceiling. He always hoped explaining would be easy. Okay, he said, I don't every day go around thinking of myself as a person who's been to Turkey, say, or France or Canada, and yet I have, right? The experiences are there—or the memories are—but I'm not constantly, you know, reviewing them. When something comes up, though, when I hear about, I don't know, street protests in Istanbul or whatever, I think, I was there. I walked through that square. I believe I had sage tea not far from there.

The man nodded in a vague fashion. Not agreeing, necessarily, but rather just indicating that he was still following along.

Of course, the husband said, the other side to all this is that I attach dates to my memories. If you said you were going to be in Turkey, I'd tell you I went, but I'd preface everything by saying, You know, it was quite a few years ago now. Which is just to say, these places change. Some customs no doubt remain the same, but how much help could I really be? Maybe the hotel where I stayed is gone, or it's called something different, ever since the one international chain bought up the other. And the places I went, that I really liked, that one jewelry shop next to the restaurant that had those great feta and basil sandwiches, it's boarded up now. Nobody knows what happened to it. If I were to go again, I might be just as lost as when I first arrived.

You know, the man said, earlier, what I was saying. I hope I didn't—

211

The husband raised his hands, palms out. It's not a problem, he said.

All right, the man said. Good. He paused, looking at the sofa. He picked something small off the fabric and dropped it on the carpet. Because I can see, he said, how it might be weird.

It's not, though, the husband said.

The man nodded. I have this dream, he said. He glanced at the husband. This isn't going to be weird.

The husband had his doubts. Tell me it's not about my wife, he said.

It's not about your wife.

All right, the husband said.

So I have this regular dream, the man said, where I'm in the middle of a strange city. Enormous buildings are all around me. There aren't streets or parks. There aren't even blocks to speak of. It's just all buildings, and they're all packed together. It's so crowded, all there are are these narrow spaces between the buildings that a person could, conceivably, squeeze through, and I do mean squeeze. Anyway, what I'm doing in the dream varies, but I always have to get something done, and it's nothing terribly exciting. Maybe I'm looking for a book, or I have this form that everyone's riding me to complete. One time, I was selling teacups, like toy teacups, for children, with their names painted on them by hand. But whatever I'm doing, it's just almost impossible in the space that is available. When I had my teacup business, I eked out this little area at the corner of a building. Another building across the way came jutting out toward me, as close as the coffee table is to the sofa, to give you some idea. That's what I have to work with. And it's so dark, too. Hardly any light gets down between the buildings. But so I'm trying to run my teacup business, and a couple of people are buying them, actually, but there's a guy selling loose batteries just a few inches away, and he's really loud, you know. He has this salesman's patter going about his batteries. You know, Fresh batteries. Three for five dollar. Three for five dollar. Something like that. Except he's much louder. And incessant. So incessant it's hard to think. And he's pushy, this battery guy. He gets up into my space and, little by little, he spreads his batteries out so they're right next to my teacups. Well, I'm no good at this. I back down. Which maybe I shouldn't do, but so be it. I give him some room, what room I have. Now the corner of the building is pressing into my shoulder. I bump my head on it. I have no more room to move.

The man turned the television off and looked at the husband. I told my father about that dream once, he said.

How did that go? the husband asked.

The man shrugged. I wouldn't recommend it.

The Admiral doesn't seem like he'd be big on dream analysis, the husband said. I mean, from what you've told me.

No, the man said. He's not.

So what did he say?

Well, the man said, he asked me what I thought it meant, and I told him.

Which was what?

The man sighed. I told him that's sort of what I think living is like, in a way. For us, I mean. For you and me, people like us, today. We're here, crowded in by all these old buildings, and we're supposed to be building new buildings, except it's so dark, who can even get any work done? There are just so many buildings already here, standing.

The husband nodded. Okay, he said. I can see that.

The man looked at the television, at the dark face of the thing.

And the Admiral didn't like that? the husband asked.

Oh, you know, the man said, he just told me never to quit or give up, to always keep trying, some bullshit like that.

Maybe he just didn't know what to tell you, the husband said.

He could have said what he said to just about anybody, about almost anything.

I'm sure he meant well, though, the husband said.

Everybody means well, the man said. That's no big thing, really, is it?

The husband said he supposed not.

I told him, too, that it was all a bunch of bullshit, the man said. I was really pissed.

I don't know, the husband said. He doesn't sound like a bad guy. To me, I mean.

My father told me to stop pitying myself, the man said. That's a direct quote, almost. He said self-pity was a disgusting trait. Work on it.

The husband nodded.

The thing is, the man said, I hadn't said anything about quitting. I wasn't talking about quitting, whatever that means. I was just trying to tell him something—something important, I thought—and he had to go and make it about quitting.

The husband said, Well, and then he didn't say anything more.

Anyway, the man said. See you tomorrow, I guess. Or later today. Whatever it is.

The husband placed his hands on his knees and looked at his feet. Then he stood. He thought for a second about asking the man was he all right, was everything, you know, okay, but he didn't know how exactly to put it. He could say it, but he wasn't sure he would say it right. Good night, he said.

The man tidied and picked up a little. He straightened a pile of magazines and then looked around the living room to see was there anything he was missing or something he should do. While he worked, he thought over what he had said about this dream of his and what it might mean, if mean was the correct word, even. He checked it for the fatal false note. He'd had ideas like this before. Big thoughts, he called them, which he meant disparagingly, because who was he kidding, really? He would not, however, talk himself out of it, not this time. Even if it wasn't actually a big thought, it was his, and he refused to take it back. Nor would he think, as he often did, But then what do I know? There was no more point in self-deprecation. There simply was no time. That was the problem—and here the man included all his friends, and all the woman's friends, everyone their age or thereabouts. The problem with them all was they had done so much of that disingenuous shuffling about, the aw-shucksing, the pay no attention to me, I'm crazy or drunk or stupid routine, that they had precious little self left. And what had they ever got in exchange? Anything? They had apologized when they shouldn't have, when they didn't even mean it. They had mocked themselves, not because they deserved a good deflating but because they were afraid, more than anything else, of being criticized. They had begged—begged—not to be taken seriously. And so now what? What next? The man didn't know. He wasn't being disingenuous, he really didn't know. They just couldn't go on as they'd been going on. That was the main thing. The man did know that.

THE HUSBAND LAY in his bed again, looking over at his wife. Outside, he heard birds already, the first of the day, and then a motorcycle passed slowly by. His wife had not stirred or made a sound when he came into the room and took off his clothes. And later, when he got up once more and went to her, to lie in her bed, because he missed her and wanted to sleep with her, no matter how little room he had or how uncomfortable he was, she did not move. The husband wrapped an arm around his wife and cupped her stomach with his hand. It seemed no larger and no different than it had the night before or the night before that, but then, he guessed, it wouldn't, not yet. As he held her, he thought of the child, their child. We will love you, he thought, but we're not ready yet. He sang this in his head, repeating it. We will love you, but we're not ready yet. It sounded like an old lost song, like in the blues, the way the first part was so sunny and certain, but then the second part let the gloom in, the wind picking up, the clouds rolling over the sun. What the first part gave, the second took back, like a thief with a knife who had pretended to be a friend. But a curious thing happened. As the husband repeated the words, he thought of moving the furniture in their house to make room for not one but two babies. He found a place for a dresser, a changing table, and two cribs. Two cribs! He could hardly believe it himself, but they were there, and they looked good. Such sturdy things. He cleaned bottles and lined them up on a shelf. Then he stored a box of diapers under his desk. He was making preparations. He was getting ready. It was all spelled out. It all seemed so clear. He installed two car seats in the back of their car and, in the next instant, he saw them all driving somewhere, his wife driving and himself riding beside her, just as they had when coming to the beach, just as they always had. When one of the babies—the boy baby, for they were girl and boy in his mind—started to cry, the husband turned around in his seat and stuck his finger inside the baby's diaper, like a dipstick, to check what was going on. That's what one is supposed to do, isn't it? The husband wasn't sure. He would find out. Whatever it was, he would learn. The husband turned back around. We need to stop, he said to his wife. He needs changing. And then the children grew older. He called the girl to come downstairs. Come play your guitar for Daddy, he said, and she appeared there, at the top of the steps, with a red guitar, kid-sized. He watched his wife teach the children Arabic or Chinese, the husband wasn't sure what it was, some language he had no hope of learning. They all sat in the living room. It was their living room, just as it already was, but they were watching dubbed cartoons and, for whatever reason, this thought, the mere picture of his wife, bent near their children, speaking to them slowly, repeating words, laughing, pointing to their hair, their eyes, their fingers and toes, and then pronouncing the new words, this thought squeezed tears from his eyes. He was sitting on the sofa, listening, watching, playing along some. He felt delirious. That's what he would have to call it. The boy brought him a purple plastic horse, and the husband said to his wife, What is the word for horse? She told him, and then he tried to repeat it. The word felt strange in his mouth, as if he had a marble on his tongue. He galloped the horse across his legs and up his body, right into his shirt pocket. Where's the horse? he said. He opened his hands, empty, and the boy pointed at his pocket. The horse was peeking out, and the boy called to it. Horse, he said. Horse. The boy wanted the horse. The wanting didn't need to be spoken. Whatever the boy said, whatever his sister said, whether it was horse or milk or book or ball, the wanting was always clear. They understood.

PARABLE OF THE BIRDS

THE MAN WAS doing chores when he noticed the first baby bird. His little boy was with him, in his arms, held against his hip. The boy was at this stage where he liked to help out with whatever his dad was doing. All the man had to say was, You want to go to the basement? Daddy needs to advance the laundry. That's what the man said, advance the laundry. He wasn't sure why he started saying it that way. He pictured a pawn advancing across a crowded chessboard. All he meant was he needed to take the stuff in the dryer and put it onto the folding table and move the stuff in the washer to the dryer, and then start washing the next load. That was how he advanced the laundry.

So the man had said to his little boy, Do you want to go to the garage? Daddy needs to take the garbage out. And, of course, the boy did. He ran to his father as if he had just been asked if he wanted an ice-cream cone. The man picked the boy up, and then they got the garbage ready. It was Sunday. Sunday was the day he took out the garbage. Monday, for the little boy, was the day the garbage trucks came. Monday was also for music class. Tuesday was the day the milkman came. The other days had not yet acquired firm identities.

After they set the garbage cans in the alley, the man decided he should do the recycling and the compost, too. Just to get it all done. He carried the little boy back up the stairs and told him what they were going to do next. He was always telling the boy what was about to happen or what had just transpired. That was when the man noticed the baby bird. It was lying on one of the steps, on its side. Its feet were pulled up under it, as if clutching something to its chest, and its beak hung partway open. The man was pretty sure the bird was dead. Flies were already buzzing around it.

The man and the little boy went inside. He washed their hands and then put his son down. Can you play with Mommy? he said. For a little bit? The man wasn't sure when he started phrasing so much of what he said to his son as a question. Like it was all optional.

In the living room, the man's wife was going through the week's junk mail, all the catalogs and come-ons that had piled up. Sometimes something decent slipped in.

So, the man said, there's a b-i-r on the steps out there. I need to clean it up. The man and his wife only ever spelled the first three letters of words, mostly the nouns, because the boy knew a lot of nouns already. Three letters were usually enough. Context was everything.

You mean, it's—

Yeah, he said. A baby, too. Their son knelt on the floor, playing with his cars. He lined them up and then tried to balance his people on top of them.

I don't think he saw it, the man said. I doubt he'd understand, but I didn't want to, you know, make a big scene.

The man got a shovel and some gloves and a couple of plastic grocery bags and went back outside. Flies crawled over the bird, more thickly than before, and the man swatted at them with his gloves. He felt angry at the flies, as if, somehow, they were to blame. He slid the bird onto the shovel and thought he heard a chirp. He stopped and looked at the bird. The edge of the shovel gleamed. It couldn't have been the bird. His bird was dead. He looked again, checking for some sign of life, some movement or breathing or anything, but he saw nothing. Then he heard another chirp. It sounded close by, somewhere, but it was not his bird. Definitely not his bird, he thought.

He eased the bird into one of the bags and tied a knot with the handles. There were ants on the step where the bird had been, all massed together in one intense spot. Could the bird have even been dead for longer than an hour? The man placed the bird inside the second bag and knotted it as well. He just didn't want anything coming for the bird, some cat or rat or the man didn't know what.

When the man returned from the alley, he found a second bird, lying at the foot of the stairs. Another baby, and the same type by the look of it. The flies were back, too, and, the man suspected, the ants as well. If they weren't, they soon would be. What was worse, though, was the bird was still alive, if only just barely. Every few seconds, it flexed its legs out and then pulled them in.

Oh no, the man said. Like he was a child. That's what the little boy said when he dropped a toy or spilled his juice all over the place.

The man wasn't sure what kind of bird it was. He'd seen them around. They had dark brown feathers and speckles across their back. He thought maybe they were grackles, but he really wasn't sure. He didn't know all the types of birds and what people called them.

The man swatted at the flies with his shovel and then looked at the bird. He rested the shovel against the steps and then folded his gloves over the handle. Where were all these birds coming from? A tree grew in their backyard, a maple, taller than their home, but the man scanned the branches and could find no nest. He looked at their house then. There were, it seemed, openings under the eaves, just beneath the gutter. The man had never noticed them before. It looked like a mistake, something left off in construction, the kind of thing he should have fixed years before. They weren't large, these openings, but he guessed they were large enough, weren't they? He looked again at the bird. Poor thing, he thought. All skin and fuzz and bald on the head. The bones of its wings were visible. The bird moved.

Oh no, the man said. Oh no. He couldn't stop saying oh no. He hurried up the steps and went inside.

His wife and the little boy were playing at a game they called bee in the box. The rules were vague and ever-evolving, but basically, there was a bee, and it could get stuck in a box, except sometimes, it could fly right out of the box and buzz around the boy or land on his head or shoulder. The bee could also walk along the edge of the box, singing its bee song, only to fall right back into the box again. The boy loved this game.

So, the man said, there's another b-i-r out there.

Really?

Yeah, and this one's alive. Sort of. I think.

His wife went back to playing. She was the bee, it seemed. Is there anything you can do? she said.

I don't think I can nurse it back to health, the man said. I mean, not in the condition it's in.

His wife nodded. Okay, she said.

I think I should probably—you know, he said. But I really don't want to do that.

It's okay, she said.

The man walked to the kitchen and looked out the window into the backyard. The bird was there still, on the ground. He thought he saw it move.

Why don't you wait an hour? his wife said. Just give it a little time. Maybe it will be fine, you never know.

The man doubted very much the bird would be fine, but it sounded good, waiting an hour.

His wife buzzed the bee around their little boy's head. The bee is getting so sleepy, she told him. Her buzzing became sluggish and then it became soft, like a whisper. The bee needs a nap, she said.

No, the boy said.

Are you sure? his wife said. She buzzed louder now.

No, the boy said.

IN THE DAYS BEFORE their child was born, just a couple of days, in fact, before they went to the hospital, a baby bird showed up on their doorstep. It could not have been more literally so. They were just sitting in the living room, watching television, when the man heard the bird.

Did you hear that? he said.

Hear what?

The man went to the door and opened it, and the bird was right there. A tiny thing, crying. It was storming out, and raining rather hard. The man figured the bird had been knocked from its nest. Maybe their doorstep, narrow as it was and barely covered, was the best shelter the bird could find.

The man bent to look at the bird. It tilted its head back and opened its beak, then it cried again.

The man closed the door. There's a bird right outside our door, he said.

There is? his wife said. She got up to come see. She was hugely pregnant and lovely. She moved about slowly, holding onto the sofa while she walked, bracing herself against the back. One of her ankles had been bothering her for the last week. They had gone to see an acupuncturist but it only helped some. She was so tired and lovely.

The bird had moved to the top of the stairs and was huddled underneath the railing.

I think I should do something, the man said. To help it.

His wife sat back down. I'm too tired to do anything, she said. But you do something.

I just think I should, the man said. I mean, it's too weird, right? Waiting for our baby and here this bird comes along. It's weird, you know?

His wife agreed it was pretty weird.

The man got an umbrella and some twine and tied the umbrella to the railing, so that it covered the bird and part of the doorstep. Then he got a shallow bowl and filled it with water. He just hoped the bird knew what to do.

I don't think I can feed it, he said.

His wife told him that was okay.

I mean, what does it even eat? the man said. Regurgitated cricket or worm or something?

I'm sure what you've done will help, his wife said.

They watched some more television. Somebody was running this marathon of a sitcom his wife had seen when she was a little girl. She knew all the jokes and how all the stories ended.

Can you rub my feet? she said.

The man took her feet into his lap. Of course he could, he said.

In the morning, the bird was gone. The man looked around for it but didn't see it anywhere, not under their steps or in their yard or in their neighbors' yards. He didn't even see any feathers on the ground. He was afraid, actually, he would find feathers. He brought the bowl inside and collapsed the umbrella, and he told his wife the news.

That night, the bird returned. Just as before, the man heard it and went to the door. He bent close, and the bird tilted its head back and cried.

Hey, the man said. Do you want some water?

He went to get a bowl, the same one as before. It's our bird, he told his wife.

He set the bowl down and then sat in the doorway. The bird

looked better maybe, a little fuller perhaps. The man wasn't sure. They look so rough when they're new.

The next morning, the bird was gone again. The man picked up the bowl and emptied the water onto a plant. As he had before, he looked around to make sure the bird hadn't fallen, or worse. He thought he heard a bird that sounded like his bird, but he couldn't be certain. It was coming from a tree, up high. He craned his neck and he shielded his eyes but he didn't see a thing.

WHILE THE LITTLE BOY NAPPED, the man went to check on the second baby bird. It was pretty much where he had left it and not looking at all well. He swatted away the flies. Stupid bird, he thought. Stupid, stupid bird. Would there be more? The man had to wonder. How many might still be hatching under the roof?

As he scooted the bird onto the shovel, its legs stretched out, as if trying to grasp his fingers. Nerves, the man thought. Just nerves. Life's last gasp or whatever. If the bird was alive somehow, if it was, in some dim, barely functioning capacity, still alive, it wouldn't be for long. The man thought he should kill the bird, probably, that it was the right thing to do, but he couldn't, not with his hands and not with the shovel's edge. He just couldn't do it. He was, he supposed, a coward. Also, he was lazy. Even if he had noticed those openings under the roof, he wouldn't likely have fixed them. He would have meant to get to the job, sure—he had good intentions— but he doubted he ever would. He wanted to be honest.

The man eased the bird into a bag. Before tying it, he forced as much air out as he could. If the bird were to suffocate, please let it die quickly, he thought. At least let it be quick.

When the little boy awoke from his nap, they went to see some trucks. The city had a thing where, every year, they brought a bunch of trucks out, parked them by the old stadium, and then let kids clamber all over them. It was something to do. They had dump trucks, diggers, bulldozers, and forklifts. There were ambulances and fire engines, garbage trucks and police cruisers. The little boy liked best the garbage trucks.

In the corner of the parking lot, families stood in a wide ring around a helicopter. The man held the little boy in his arms, against his hip, and his wife took photographs. Soon, the main rotor on top of the helicopter began to turn, slowly at first and then faster, until it was chopping the air, and all the man could hear was the heavy, regular beat of the blades.

Inside, two men readied themselves, checking controls, whatnot.

The man pointed at the helicopter. Do you see the men? he said. They're wearing helmets. The little boy had just learned the word helmet. The man pointed to his head. Helmet, he said. He wasn't sure the boy could hear him. He was shouting and he hardly heard himself.

The helicopter rose up, hovering a few feet off the ground. Dust filled the air, and the man covered his child's eyes. The helicopter floated before them, bobbing slightly, like a toy. It rotated to the right and then back to the left. The man started to cry a little. He had no idea why. It wasn't the dust, he knew. As the helicopter took to the air, he kissed the back of his boy's head and held him tightly. They watched the helicopter pass overhead and then circle around the stadium. People waved, cheered, pointed at the sky.

THE CRYING wasn't a big thing, but it did perplex the man. One night, a few days after the fact, he asked his wife if she happened to remember the helicopter.

Of course she did, she said. Why?

That's when he told her something had come over him. That was how he put it. They were reading in bed. His wife was lying backwards, facing the headboard, with her legs resting against the wall. It was some stretching exercise she did. For circulation, the man thought. He couldn't remember now, she had been doing it since before the baby.

His wife thought maybe it was just because their boy had enjoyed the helicopter. He was so excited, she said. To see his face, the look on it.

The man wasn't sure. It was like, watching the helicopter with him, he said, I saw it as he would see it, maybe. Or anyway, how I imagined he might see it. The man riffled the pages of his magazine. It all seemed, suddenly, too much somehow. It seemed like such a strange place, he said. The world and this thing in it, flying, and us there. And why was any of it there? Why were we there, you know, watching?

We went for the trucks, his wife said. Because he really likes trucks.

Right, I know, the man said, but can you imagine never having seen something fly before, and then, right there in front of you, this thing flies?

I don't know, his wife said. He looked happy to me.

That's good, I guess, the man said. He stroked his wife's legs while she stretched. He was thinking back on the time, trying not just to remember it, but seeing if he couldn't feel what he had felt. He had this idea that if he could feel it again, then he might be able to understand it this time. He could move through it slowly, patiently viewing it frame by frame, pausing, rewinding, and then playing it back once more. But already, the experience had dimmed. It was like looking at a beloved painting hung behind a thick pane of glass.

Maybe it just scared me, the man said. He looked over at his wife. She was paging rapidly through her magazine, as if hunting for something she knew had to be there. Do you ever get like that? he said.

She stopped flipping. Like what?

The man put his hands behind his head and looked at the ceiling. How to explain? It's like, he said, but then he stopped, because maybe, he thought, he should just bail, make an easy joke and scurry away. He could think about it later—or not. Whichever, it didn't matter. Somewhere, a rare tree stood in the middle of a meadow on an island that the man had glimpsed only a few times from the sea. The point was to get there. The only problem was he didn't know how, not always.

It's like there's some basic thing, the man said at last, some basic, fundamental thing, but when you think of it, it's scary now. It's not basic anymore, it's inconceivable or it's strange or it's whatever. But the thing is, he said, you've never given it any thought before, you never bothered, because why would you? And now, of course, now you can't stop. You just keep thinking of the stupid thing.

The man turned to his wife. Do you know what I mean? he said.

His wife thought for a second. There was this one time, she said. I was climbing some stairs. I worked in an office, on the sixth floor of a building. This was years ago, she said. This was before I met you. I thought it was good exercise, you know, taking the stairs. They were on the outside of the building. They were glassed in, but you could see out, so there was a view. I really liked that view. I liked to look down at the people as I walked up the stairs. I'd pick someone out and then I'd try to keep that person in my sight. Anyway, one day, in the middle of climbing, I was, I don't know, four flights up maybe, when I thought, How am I doing this? The climbing, I meant. How does it even work? I took another step then and I almost fell. My foot felt weird, like it wasn't my foot. I couldn't control it. It wouldn't go up, at least not as far as I needed it to. And the next step was just as awkward. I had to will my feet to move. I had to concentrate and really focus on what I was doing. First the one foot, and then the other. I was telling myself that. It was like I'd never climbed stairs before. Finally, I just had to stop. I sat down against the railing and I rested.

What did you do? the man asked.

Eventually, I got up. I had to.

But about the stairs, the man said.

I made it the rest of the way, she said. Somehow.

And later? he said. After that?

Well, she said, I guess, for a while, stairs seemed rather odd to me.

FENCE BOOKS

NATIONAL POETRY SERIES

The Network — Jena Osman

The Black Automaton — Douglas Kearney

Collapsible Poetics Theater — Rodrigo Toscano

ANTHOLOGIES & CRITICAL WORKS

Not for Mothers Only: Contemporary Poets on Child-Getting & Child-Rearing — Catherine Wagner & Rebecca Wolff, editors

A Best of Fence: *The First Nine Years,* Volumes 1 & 2 — Rebecca Wolff and *Fence* Editors, editors

POETRY

June — Daniel Brenner

English Fragments/A Brief History of the Soul — Martin Corless-Smith

The Sore Throat & Other Poems — Aaron Kunin

Dead Ahead — Ben Doller

My New Job — Catherine Wagner

Stranger — Laura Sims

The Method — Sasha Steensen

The Orphan & Its Relations — Elizabeth Robinson

Site Acquisition — Brian Young

Rogue Hemlocks — Carl Martin

19 Names for Our Band — Jibade-Khalil Huffman

Infamous Landscapes — Prageeta Sharma

Bad Bad — Chelsey Minnis

Snip Snip! — Tina Brown Celona

Yes, Master — Michael Earl Craig

MALIS   IFICW
Maliszewski, Paul.
Prayer and parable :[stories] /

CENTRAL LIBRARY
10/11